SHOOTOUT AT THE SNAKE PIT

A Jesse Garnett Western

R. Annan

One Vision Publishing

Shootout at the Snake Pit
Copyright 2017 by R. Annan
WGA Reg. #: R32144 (1/30/17)

Author's Portrait: Hazel Tertsakian
Editor: Karren Doll Tolliver
Photography © L. Annan

One Vision Publishing
Published 2017
ISBN: 978-1-942338-67-3 (Print Book)
ISBN: 978-1-942338-68-0 (eBook)

Western books by R. Annan

Fight for the Lazy M
The Red Bandana
The Salvation of Trace Logan
The Cowboy from Sierra Blanca

Jack Cordell Westerns

The Gunfighter in Winter
Long Ride to Hell's Kitchen
Owl Hawks
Gunfight at Barfield Springs
Shootout at Sanctuary City
Last Days of a Gunfighter

Clay Jared Westerns

Copperhead Moon
Cowboys of the Box R
Prisoners of Brimstone Pass
Range War in C Minor
Devil Wind
Showdown at Wamego Falls
Lightning Riders
Winter Kill
Gunfight at Wild River
Shootout at Rattlesnake Flats

Jesse Garnett Westerns

Gunfight at Black Bear Lair
Gunfight at Latigo Junction
Outcasts of Troublesome Creek

Dedication

To

Karren Doll Tolliver

Chapter 1

Ram Harper and his boys rode into Easton's Corners on a Monday morning intending to rob the town's bank. Harper figured the town would be sleepy and exhausted. Most cow towns were like that on a Monday morning. Cowboys came from the ranches on Friday and whooped it up until late Sunday night. After a wild weekend, out of money and pie eyed, they rode back to their ranches, groaning and slumped over their saddles, leaving a beat up town behind. From experience, Ram Harper knew Monday morning was usually the best time to rob a bank.

After hanging around town for a week, observing the comings and goings, Harper quickly figured out that Easton's Corners Cattlemen's Bank had a large amount of money. At least thirty thousand dollars was there for the taking. And, best of all, the only lawman in town was a bowlegged old marshal who was most likely afraid of his own shadow.

1

As for Harper's men, they were all professionals. Early in their lives, they had been cowboys and could shoot straight and ride hard. Tired of sleeping out nights and eating chuck, they exchanged their quarter horses for mustangs and rode the outlaw trail with Harper. The plan was to rob the bank and head for Sharon Springs. There was a robber's hideout near there called the Snake Pit. From the Snake Pit, it was a short ride into Colorado and Cheyenne Wells.

The first to ride into town was Hugh Mason. He rode slowly up the main street and stopped in front of Becker's Beanery, two doors past the bank. Dismounting, Mason sat on the porch steps and began whittling on a piece of wood. As he whittled, he looked up and down the street. The banks were getting smarter. They were posting guards on rooftops, in alleyways and in empty buildings. It was Mason's job to watch for that. This morning he saw none and that made him feel good.

Next, Kinsey Blue rode slowly into town on a chestnut colored mustang with a star on its forehead. He tied up at the loading dock in front of Morgan's Mercantile, across from the bank. There was one horse tied at the rail, which meant there was only one customer in the mercantile.

Sitting on the loading dock, Blue took a piece of thin, five foot long rawhide out of his shirt pocket. He tied a honda knot to one end, made a small loop, did a quick over under over with the honda knot and formed a small lasso. He chuckled and toyed with the lasso, twirling it around. Never once did the outlaw take his eyes off the street or rooftops.

Harper arrived with Wade Downy and Sam Meany. The trio stopped at Delmar's Saddle and Gun Repair Shop, three doors away from the bank. Harper got a small paper bag from his saddlebags. It had a rag stuffed inside. Since Harper was a stranger, the suspicious minded guard at the door stopped him.

"What's in thet bag, mister?"

"Money. I'm makin' a deposit, friend."

"Mind if I take a look, mister?"

"Not at all, friend," Harper replied. As Harper took his time opening the bag, Downy came up behind the guard and put the barrel of his gun against his back.

"Let's go inside, friend," Harper said calmly, smiling at the guard.

The guard knew he'd been tricked and wasn't going to die for the bank. He nodded, turned and led Harper and Downy inside. Meany came in behind them. Once inside, Meany pulled a piece of rawhide from his pocket, tied the guard's hands behind him and had him sit on the floor in a corner. Harper discarded the paper bag and held his gun to the bank manager's head. The teller, a frightened old woman, filled a bank sack full of money from the cash drawer and safe.

Everything went as planned, and within fifteen minutes they were out on the street. Harper whistled loudly, signaling to Blue and Mason it was time to go. They all mounted up quickly and rode out of town at a fast clip. A few townsfolk stood looking on and wondering what the big hurry was. A dog chased after them but it soon came back panting with its tongue hanging out.

The outlaws were well out of town when Harper glanced back and noticed that Blue was towing another horse behind him. A girl sat in the saddle with her hands tied to the horn with a piece of rawhide. She struggled to get loose. As they came to a stand of pine trees, Harper rode in and the others followed. When they were deep into the trees, the outlaw chief stopped them and stared at Blue and the girl. He noticed she was dressed in riding clothes, like the kind those English ladies wore when they rode with the hounds.

"What's going on, Blue? Who the heck is this?"

"It's a girl."

"I can see that, but what the heck are you doing with her?"

"She came outta the mercantile an' smiled at me," Blue said. He had a crazed, idiotic smirk on his face. "So, heck, I jest took her."

"What the hell for, Blue?"

"Like I told ya, Ram, because she smiled at me," Blue replied. He chuckled insanely as he glared at the girl. She strained to get her hands loose, staring hatefully at him. "She's the prettiest darn thing I ever did see. Ain't she pretty, Ram?"

"Yeah, she's pretty alright, but whatta ya gonna do with her?"

"I'm gonna keep her. She's somethin' special," Blue said eagerly. "Look how she's dressed, all fancy in thet ridin' outfit, like in the magazine pictures."

Harper's face hardened. "You crazy fool," he growled, "you'll have us all hung!"

"Aw, they ain't gonna catch us, Ram," Blue whined, like a little child.

Harper turned to the girl. "Who are you?"

"Lacey Garth," the girl said with stubborn authority. If she was afraid, it didn't show. "My father is Theodore Garth. My mother is Sandra Garth. They're important people around here. You'd better release me or you're all going to hang!"

Harper looked at Blue. "Cut her loose. She's trouble. Do it now, you damn crazy fool!" The outlaw chief shook his head in disbelief and rode on.

He was thirty feet away when Blue yelled, "Ta hell I will!"

The outlaw chief yanked his mount to a sudden stop and reined it around in Blue's direction. "What did you just say?"

"I said I ain't gonna give her up, Ram!"

"Are you bracing me, Blue?"

"Maybe. What if I am?"

"Then you better draw!" Ram Harper growled and went for his gun.

Before the outlaw chief got his weapon clear, Blue drew and fanned off two shots hitting Harper in the chest, and knocking him from the saddle to the ground. Blue quickly turned his gun on the others.

"Jesus," Mason said, "You jest kilt the boss!"

"I guess this makes me the boss, now, don't it, Mason?" Blue said in a high pitched, crazed voice. His face was flushed and his eyes bulged with excitement.

Downy, Mason and Meany looked at each other and shrugged. They were thinking mostly of the money and the posse that was being formed back in town. The girl was strictly Blue's worry. He'd get rid of her after he had some fun with her down the line. She wasn't their problem.

"I'm ridin'," Mason said to Blue. "Do what ya wanna do."

"I damn sure will," Blue said with a broad smile. He grabbed the saddlebags with the money from Harper's horse, dropped it over the neck of his mount and rode off, towing the girl behind him. He knew they'd have to follow him because he had the money. They had no choice. He was faster on the draw than any of them, and they knew it.

He was also as crazy as a fox.

Chapter 2

It was a clear, crisp, sunny day in April when Jesse Garnett was ambushed fifteen miles outside of Easton's Corners. He'd been on the road for three days and was half asleep in the saddle when they caught him by surprise. The big appaloosa sensed it was coming and started blowing, but by then it was too late.

Garnett took a blow on the back of the head that knocked him half unconscious to the ground. His two attackers dragged his body into the trees next to the road, then took his gunbelt, gun, pocket money, and horse.

Not satisfied with hitting him over the head with a tree limb, they shot him as well. It was a wild, hasty shot that hit Garnett just below the left rib cage. He had sense enough to play dead. They rode off in a cloud of dust on Garnett's big appaloosa, one in the saddle and one behind the cantle. The leader wore a Confederate army jacket and hat, while his companion wore rags. They both smelled strongly of sweat and tobacco.

After they were out of sight, Garnett sat up with a groan, opened his shirt, and looked at his wound. The bullet had cut a grove in the flesh on his left side. It was just below the one he got about a year, in Latigo Junction. This new wound was hardly bleeding and a crust was already forming. It didn't hurt as much as the blow on his head did.

"Get the hell up and get going!" Garnett muttered to himself. "Do something even if it's wrong!" He started to chuckle but ended up painfully sucking air. Grabbing a low hanging tree branch, he pulled himself to his feet and leaned against the trunk. "You're fine," he said out loud, as if talking to a friend. "Just get moving and you'll be alright."

The ex-outlaw walked along at a slow, halting pace, holding his side. After traveling about a hundred yards, he sat down in the middle of the road to rest. "Jesse, old pal," he said, speaking to himself again, "this ain't gonna work out. Maybe you should just go lay under a tree and die proper, like."

The sound of an approaching horse got his attention. Glancing back, Garnett saw a rider coming up behind him. The rider saw him, too, and stopped about thirty feet away. It was a young cowboy on a dun quarter horse. He sat in the saddle with a curious smirk on his face, staring in Garnett's direction.

"What the hell you doin' down there, ol' man, sayin' yer prayers?" the cowboy yelled at him.

"I just got robbed by two bushwhackers, sonny," Garnett moaned.

The cowboy laughed. "Well, thet ain't right, now, is it, old man?"

"Don't call me old man," Garnett said.

"Don't call me sonny."

"Alright, mister," Garnett replied sarcastically.

"An' don't call me mister, either," the cowboy said.

Garnett sighed in frustration. "What the heck do you want me to call you?"

"Call me Rick. Rick Pruitt."

"Okay, Rick Pruitt!" Garnett was getting irritated.

The young cowboy walked his horse alongside Garnett and stared down at him. "Jesus! Yer shot, aincha?"

"Do you always talk so much, kid?"

"Where'd them bushwhackers go, mister?"

"Down the road. They got my horse and gun. About a half hour ago."

The cowboy leaned over the side of his horse and stretched out his hand to Garnett. "Hop on, old timer."

Garnett grabbed his hand and got up on his feet. The cowboy gave him the left stirrup and Garnett swung up behind the cantle. Once they were settled in, the cowboy got the dun moving.

"What's yer name, mister?" Pruitt asked. Garnett was glad he had dropped the old timer bit.

"Garnett. Jesse Garnett."

"Howdy, Garnett."

"Thanks for the lift, Pruitt."

"Hang on," Pruitt said as he nudged the horse into a lope.

"They won't get far," Garnett replied. "Once my horse gets a good whiff of them he'll stop dead. He won't budge. He's funny that way."

Pruitt laughed. "He is, huh? Thet's sure one smart horse."

"Yeah. He's pretty smart."

A mile ahead, the road made a dogleg to the left. They followed it around and saw Garnett's appaloosa standing in the road complaining to the two men on its back. The man with the Confederate jacket sat in the saddle, kicking the big appaloosa in the barrel, trying to get it moving. Suddenly it squealed in pain and fishtailed hard up and to the right. Both riders went flying in the air, hitting the road with a thud. As they struggled up, they noticed Garnett and Pruitt.

"Looks like we got company, Ben," the one in rags said.

"It's jest some kid, Tom," the one in the Confederate jacket replied, drawing the gun he had taken from Garnett. He thumbed the hammer back. "Come in closer, sonny, with yer hands away from yer gun."

"What for?" Pruitt asked calmly.

"So I kin drill yer ass, thet's why."

"Go ahead, friend," Pruitt said. "You kin have first shot."

"I'll jest take thet offer," Ben replied.

13

Ben took aim and fired off a shot. It narrowly missed the cowboy. Garnett flinched as the bullet snapped past his head. The kid was unusually calm.

"My turn," Pruitt said.

He drew and fanned off a return shot, hitting the outlaw in the chest, knocking him flat on his back on the road. His pal turned and ran into the woods.

"Jesus, kid," Garnett said, as he slid to the ground. "You got a death wish or something?"

Pruitt smiled and said, "Nope. A fortuneteller in Stockton told me I'd die in the arms of a beautiful woman. An' you sure ain't no beautiful woman, Garnett."

It was Garnett's turn to laugh, even though it pained him. He walked over to the dead man and took his gunbelt, gun, and pocket money back. The appaloosa came over and nuzzled him.

"You okay, pal?" Garnett asked as he inspected the big horse carefully. "Yeah, I guess you're okay." Garnett grabbed the reins and saddle horn and said, "Down!"

Pruitt watched as the appaloosa knelt on its front legs. It waited until Garnett was in the saddle, then straightened up.

"Darn," Pruitt said. "That's one savvy bronc." He nodded at the dead man. "What about him?"

"Crow bait," Garnett said as he turned the appaloosa around and started down the road. The young cowboy rode up alongside.

"Ain't you forgotten something, old man?"

"What's that?" Garnett replied.

"Well, a thank you would be nice, since I saved yer sorry butt back there."

"I'd have done the same for you, kid."

"Yer a real old grouch, Garnett. You know that?" Pruitt said. "An' an ungrateful one ta boot."

Garnett reined his horse to a stop. He turned and looked at the young cowboy. "Okay, Pruitt, thanks for saving my sorry hide."

Pruitt stopped his dun. "You know what you need, old man? You need ta git drunk and have yer whistle cleaned. Yer about as touchy as an ol' broke back mule."

Garnett started to laugh, but grabbed his side and groaned. "Yeah, kid, yer right. Let's stop at the nearest town

15

and tie one on." As they rode along, Garnett said, "Say, kid, I knew a man in Storeyville Prison by the name of Pruitt. Any relation?"

"Nope, but we do have a sky pilot in the family," Pruitt replied. "How come you was in prison?"

"I was robbin' a bank and my horse threw me."

Pruitt laughed. "Yer one sorry ass bank robber, Garnett."

"Watch your mouth, kid," Garnett said halfheartedly, smiling. There was something familiar about the kid. His go to hell ways reminded him of himself when he was younger.

Farther up the road they saw a sign nailed to a scrub oak. It said, Easton's Corners - 6 miles.

Chapter 3

It was late afternoon when Pruitt and Garnett rode into Easton's Corners. The young cowboy peeled off at the Crazy Cow Saloon while Garnett went looking for a doctor. He found one named Samuel P. Evans in the middle of the town. Doc Evans had just finished lancing a boil on a cowboy's neck.

"I guess you're next, mister," the cowboy said to Garnett as he left.

Doc Evans was a middle aged man with thin, white hair. He snickered as he worked over Garnett's wound, thinking he'd seen that same wound a hundred times or more. Wounds like that kept him in business.

"What's so funny, Doc?" Garnett asked.

"Not a thing, my friend, not a thing."

"How much?" Garnett asked when the doc was finished wrapping him up.

"Hell, half an eagle should cover it."

Garnett paid and left. He walked his horse up the street past a bank to a place called Becker's Beanery. He had a bowl of chili and three sourdough biscuits. Finished eating, he rolled a cigarette and sat smoking over a cup of thick, black, greasy coffee. When the salty chili kicked in, he left the beanery and walked his horse down to the Crazy Cow Saloon to slake his thirst. Also, he wanted to see what kind of trouble Pruitt had gotten himself into.

Garnett walked into the saloon and bought a bottle of locally brewed beer called Hog's Breath. It was a common potato beer, flat and bitter, but it cooled the fire of the chili burning in his stomach.

"You just had some of Becker's chili, didn't you?" the barman said with a smile.

"How'd you know that?" Garnett asked.

"It shows. He sends a lot of people my way. I'm Frank Tully," the barman said. "I won the place."

"Did you say you won the place or own the place?"

"Both. I won it in a poker game, so now I own it," Tully said smugly.

"I'm Jesse Garnett," Garnett replied. They shook hands over the bar. "Did a young, snot nosed cowboy come in here?"

"Yeah," Tully said. "He's back there playing poker. He's gonna get skinned alive. That guy in the suit is a card sharp."

Garnett chuckled. "It'll teach him a lesson." He looked around and saw Pruitt at a table with four other men. The cowboy saw him, tossed in his hand and walked up front to the bar.

"Did ya find a sawbones?" Pruitt asked.

"Yep. I'm all sewed up."

"Good. Lend me some money."

"Nope."

"How come?"

"You're a lousy card player, kid, and that guy in the fancy suit is a professional."

Pruitt turned to the barman. "What's his name?"

"Heck if I know. He just showed up last night. Does a good job of cleaning out everybody he plays with, though," Tully replied.

"Well, he jest got my last eagle," Pruitt said.

At that moment they heard voices outside. They got louder as they came near. Footsteps pounded on the porch. A marshal stepped through the batwing doors and stood looking around. A woman walked in beside him. She was dressed in an expensive riding habit, the kind seen in magazines. It included a wide brimmed black hat, a light blue linen shirt, brown leather vest, jodhpurs and high leather boots. She also wore a gunbelt and gun. Garnett took her to be about forty at most. She was sweet to the eyes.

The marshal was much older than the woman was. He was tall, but bent from age, with white hair and a kindly face burnt brown from the sun. His huge hands were gnarled and calloused from use.

"Men," he said in a rusty voice, "I'm Ed Fargo, town marshal. This is Mrs. Garth. I'm gettin' up a posse ta go after her daughter. The Ram Harper gang took her yesterday afternoon outside of Morgan's Mercantile. They also took thirty thousand dollars. The bank has authorized me ta pay ten dollars a day."

Those at the tables stopped playing cards and stared at the woman. She was strikingly beautiful with long black hair and deep black eyes, and she carried herself with a bold confidence. She was aware of her effect on men.

"Is she a-comin', too, Marshal?" someone asked. The other men at the tables snickered. Of course she wasn't coming. It was too dangerous for a woman.

The woman answered for herself. "Yes, I am." She had a rich woman's voice that revealed high learning. "My daughter will need me when we find her."

The snickering quickly stopped. This woman was no fool and she wouldn't tolerate foolishness. It was obvious she was well educated, well traveled, and not to be trifled with.

"How come yer husband ain't here, ma'am?" another asked. "Seems like he should be here, not you."

"Not that it's any of your business, but my husband is in Kansas City at a cattlemen's meeting," she said flatly. The room went quiet.

"There's been a rumor goin' around about a thousand dollar reward. Is it true, ma'am?" someone else asked.

"That's right. I'll pay a thousand dollar bonus to the man or men who rescue my daughter. That's besides the ten dollars a day Marshal Fargo will pay you."

"Did you say a thousand, lady?" someone asked. The rumor had already been going around, but nobody believed it.

"Yes, a thousand dollars!"

That got their attention. A thousand dollars was big money for a cowboy, more than he could make in five years. Even a gambler would take notice of that much money.

The marshal cleared his throat. "One thing. No whiskey. I don't allow no drinkin' on the trail."

"What about supplies?" another one asked.

"Mrs. Garth will have a packhorse with food and water. Nothin' fancy, jest regular trail grub. We'll stop to eat at places on the way."

"When are we leavin'?" someone asked.

"At sunup, tomorrow," the marshal replied.

"I'll be staying in town at the hotel," Sandra Garth said. "The packhorse will be down at Dan Cooper's stable. We'll meet there at sunup."

The marshal added, "An' we're not waitin' on any latecomers, so be there on time." He looked around, and then added, "Any questions?"

"Yeah," someone in the back of the crowd asked, "since she's comin', kin I bring my girlfriend, too?"

Everyone laughed except the marshal. "No, ya can't. An' you kin fergit about comin' yerself!" With that, Sandra Garth and Marshal Fargo left the Crazy Cow Saloon.

"They're going up to Becker's Beanery to make the same pitch," Frank Tully said to Garnett.

Garnett asked, "I wonder how many will go?"

"Plenty, I'll bet," Pruitt replied, "A thousand bucks is a lot of money. I bet none of 'em has ever seen a hundred dollars all at one time."

The bartender smiled and shook his head. "Plenty? I don't think so, kid."

"Why not?" Pruitt asked.

"The Ram Harper gang is why not," Tully replied, "They're the ones who took the girl. Only a fool would go up against the Ram Harper gang. They're bad medicine. One of 'em is crazy as a loon. His name is Kinsey Blue, as I heard."

"Never heard of them or him," Pruitt said. "How about you, Garnett?"

"Nope, never heard of Harper or Blue."

"How do they know it was them, fer sure?" Pruitt asked.

"The bank manager heard one of 'em say Harper's name," Tully replied.

"Well, I don't care who it was, I ain't afraid of no outlaws," Pruitt said boastfully.

Garnett stretched and yawned. He asked the bartender, "This town got a place to sleep, Frank?"

"Down the street," Tully replied. "The Mandan Hotel. You can't miss it. It's the tallest building in town. It's got three floors."

Garnett nodded and turned to the Pruitt. "Seein' as I owe you, kid, here's some spendin' money." He dug several quarter eagles out of his pocket and handed them to Pruitt.

"Thanks paw," the young cowboy said.

"Keep talking smart to me and I'll take 'em back."

"Sorry."

Garnett finished his beer and walked his horse down to Dan Cooper's stable and blacksmith concession.

"He needs a good feeding and brushing down. Sponge his back legs down with vinegar and check his shoes," Garnett said. "He's going for a long ride and I want him in top shape."

"Don't worry," the stableman replied. "I'll fix him up good."

Garnett gave Cooper an eagle, grabbed his saddlebags, walked over to the Mandan hotel and rented a room. His body had gone through a lot and he needed rest. Before getting in bed, he laid the saddlebags under the pillow and placed his gun next to them.

There was over eight thousand dollars in secret compartments in the bags, money he had gotten in various ways by being fast with a gun. The money, come by honestly, was his stake to a better life when he decided to settle down. It was the down payment on either a mercantile, a saloon or a hotel. The only thing missing was a woman to share it with. He hadn't found the right one, but he felt he would know her when they met.

He hoped to add another thousand dollars to it by rescuing Sandra Garth's daughter.

Chapter 4

The barman was right about the four men Pruitt was playing cards with. The tall one was a card sharp, but he wasn't alone. The other three were his pals and they rode the area fleecing cowboys and unsuspecting town folk. When Sandra Garth mentioned the thousand dollar reward, Sloan Braddock, their leader, took an immediate interest in her situation. He liked what he saw, a beautiful, mature, strong willed woman. If she was his, he wouldn't ride off to a convention in Kansas City and leave her behind.

Braddock sat at the table facing his three friends. He fanned the cards smoothly and flawlessly, making them roll slowly like an ocean wave from his right hand to his left. Sam Warfield, Cass Wheeler and Lou Preston watched, waiting for their leader to say something. He finally did.

"How would you men like to get a little fresh air and pick up some extra money as well?"

"You thinkin' about joinin' that search party, boss?" Wheeler asked.

"Maybe. It has crossed my mind," Braddock replied.

Wheeler knew his boss was a charmer when it came to women. He had a way with them. They could see this one was special, high above the others Braddock had fooled around with in the past. Sandra Garth was not only beautiful, she was rich and smart. They had seen their boss work. He could trick a woman out of her money and jewelry before she even knew it was gone. It would be interesting to see Braddock work his charms on this one. It might even turn out differently. Perhaps she was his match. Maybe she would hog tie him, brand him, and toss him aside.

"Is it the money or the woman this time, boss?" Warfield asked.

"It's the woman," Braddock answered. He looked over to where Sandra had been standing by the batwings. "Did you boys get a good look at her?"

Preston laughed loudly. "We sure did, boss. She sure is something, all right. She makes them painted ladies look pretty shabby, don't she?" The others nodded in agreement.

"I wonder what she's worth," Warfield mused aloud.

Braddock gave him a look. "Whatta you mean, Sam?"

"Well, from the way she talked, her old man is one of them cattle barons. It sounded like it to me."

Braddock quickly replied, "Forget that, Warfield. Kidnapping is a risky trail ta ride."

"Yeah," Preston said. "We don't ride thet trail."

Warfield shrugged. "I was jest speculatin', is all. I didn't mean nothin'."

It was starting to get dark. Tully, the barman, went around lighting the oil lamps that hung from the rafters. A coolness was setting in, now that the sun had gone down behind the town.

Cowboys from the ranches and men from the town began coming into the Crazy Cow. Some asked to sit in. When the empty chairs were filled with warm bodies, Braddock started the game. He smiled as he dealt the cards. He had total recall and didn't cheat unless he had to. There were times when a card sharp sat in. When that happened, Braddock watched and figured out what he was up against. If the man started to cheat, Braddock knew it and waited for a

29

chance to expose him. With Warfield, Wheeler and Preston on his side, he knew he was safe. If it came to gunplay, they would cover him. Sometimes, but not very often, there would be shooting. He tried to avoid that because it usually involved a town marshal coming in and arresting someone. Braddock didn't want to get a reputation as a troublemaker.

Around midnight Braddock decided he'd had enough and decided to break up the game. He hadn't won as much as he usually did because he couldn't concentrate on the cards. The vision of Sandra Garth's face kept getting in the way and clouding his thoughts.

Later, alone with his men, Braddock said, "Let's stay overnight at the hotel."

"So, it's gonna be her, is it, boss?"

"Yeah," Braddock replied thoughtfully. "It might be interesting. You men don't have to go. You can wait here until I come back, if you want."

"No, we'll go, boss," Wheeler said. "I'd like ta see how you handle her. She ain't gonna be easy, like the others."

Braddock smiled and nodded. "No, she sure won't. I've never seen one like her before. It should be fun."

"My money is on you, boss," Preston said. "You'll have her tied an' branded before she knows what hit her." They all laughed.

Later, as they left the bar, Braddock gave Frank Tully a double eagle. It was something he always did. This way he knew he would be welcomed back. He learned early in the game never to burn his bridges behind him.

The Mandan Hotel suddenly found itself a place of interest. Owner Missy Foster signed in over a dozen new guests. She knew it was because Sandra Garth had taken a room there. Garnett had a room on the second floor. About an hour after midnight he heard a knock at his door. He quickly sat up in bed.

"Who is it?"

"Me, Rick Pruitt."

With his Colt pointed, Garnett got out of bed, walked across the room to the door and removed the chair he had jammed against it.

"Come on in," he said with a yawn. Shutting the door, he slid the chair against it again and sat down on the edge of the bed. He stared with bleary eyes at Pruitt. "Whatta ya want, kid?"

Pruitt shivered. "Funny how it gets cold so quick around here when the sun goes down."

"Is that what you came to tell me?"

"All the rooms are full. I guess I waited too long."

Garnett scratched his head and sighed. "You're broke again, aincha?"

"I reckon."

"I guess I'm stuck with you, then, ain't I?"

"Yeah, well, from the looks of some of them guys, ya might be glad ta have me around before this deal is over."

"So, you're going?"

"Yeah. The money is good."

Garnett nodded. "I had the same idea."

"How about we watch each other's backs. Jest in case."

Garnett thought about that for a quick moment. "Sure, why not?"

"Shake on it?" the young cowboy asked.

"Sure."

They shook hands. Pruitt laughed. Garnett asked, "What's so funny, kid?"

"The gambler."

"What about him?"

"He's gonna go after thet woman the first chance he gits," Pruitt said.

Garnett shrugged. "That's her problem. She's a big girl. I'm sure she can handle him."

"Maybe she's thet kind of woman."

"What kind?"

"The kind who wants a little excitement on the side."

"Well, if she does, she'll soon be getting all she can handle."

"Maybe she might need protectin'," Pruitt said.

Garnett laughed. "From who?"

"I don't know, maybe from men like the gambler."

"Kid, you got a lot to learn about women. She'll chew him up and pick her teeth with his bones. So, don't fret about her. That lady knows her way around men. You can bet on it."

They didn't speak for a while until Pruitt asked, "Can I sleep in the chair?"

"Sure, but don't snore or I'll have to shoot you."

"I never snore."

"How do you know?"

"Because no painted lady has ever said I did."

"Is that so, mister man of the world?"

"Yup."

"Well, be careful. You might fall off the chair and break your neck."

They finally gave up bantering and went to sleep. When Garnett woke up in the morning, the young cowboy was lying next to him in the bed, hogging the covers.

Chapter 5

Starting out at sunup didn't work out as planned. Marshal Fargo was half an hour late and Mrs. Garth came fifteen minutes after him. At first it looked as if they wouldn't have enough men, but Sloan Braddock showed up with Warfield, Wheeler and Preston. Then others began to arrive. Some of them looked shabby and seedy. The marshal asked them some questions, didn't like their answers and sent them on their way. With Garnett, Pruitt, Marshal Fargo, Sandra Garth, three men from town and Braddock and his crew, that gave them a total of eleven. After they had fed, watered and dressed the horses, Marshal Fargo gathered them in front of the stables to make a speech.

"Men," he said with authority, "them outlaws was last seen a-ridin' west towards Sharon Springs on the ol' coach road. There's an old outlaw hideout near there called the Snake Pit. It's between Sharon Springs and Cheyenne Wells, jest inside the Kansas line."

"I ain't goin' to no outlaw hideout," one of the men from town said. "I been ta one an' almost got kilt!"

"We won't have ta go there if we move fast," the marshal reassured him. "The girl will slow them down."

"Well, I sure hope so," the man said.

Sloan Braddock spoke up. "Let's go. We're wasting time talking." He smiled at Mrs. Garth. She returned his smile and nodded.

Braddock, Wheeler, Warfield and Preston mounted their horses and moved out, and the rest fell in behind. By then it was almost noon. Mrs. Garth rode up alongside Braddock. She sized him up, liking what she saw, a strong, handsome man who could be a leader.

"Thank you, mister," she said.

"Sloan Braddock, Mrs. Garth." Braddock tipped his hat in a salute. "Don't worry. We'll get your little girl back. My friends here are fast with a horse and a gun."

"That's comforting to know, Mr. Braddock."

"Call me Sloan, ma'am."

"Alright, Sloan. Call me Sandra."

"Alright, Sandra," Braddock replied, giving the woman his most suggestive smile. "I'm at your service, ma'am."

For a moment, he wondered if she caught his hidden meaning. Sandra nodded as a signal she understood. But before Braddock could go any further, the marshal rode up alongside them.

"You alright, Mrs. Garth?" he asked.

"Yes, Marshal, I'm fine. Mr. Braddock was just assuring me that he and his men are fully dedicated to finding my daughter."

The old marshal gave Braddock a quick, questioning glance. "Thet's good ta know, ma'am," he said. There was a hint of sarcasm in his tone. One of the men from town rode up beside the marshal. "Ma'am," the marshal said, "this is Pete Lowry. Pete is one of the best trackers around. He gonna keep us goin' in the right direction, ain't ya, Pete?"

Lowry nodded. He appeared to have Indian blood in him. His long, black hair fell almost to his waist. He grunted and rode on ahead to take the lead.

It was midafternoon when they stopped by a stream near a big cottonwood to rest the horses. They ate hardtack and jerky, washing it down with water. In an hour the marshal had them back on the trail, following Pete Lowry. Near sundown, exhausted and saddle weary, they made camp for the day. The marshal marked off a separate spot for Mrs. Garth's tent, and Braddock had Wheeler, Warfield and Preston put it up. The others gathered wood. Pete Lowry made the fire and a pot of coffee. They ate jerky and hardtack again.

Braddock and his men tossed their bedrolls close to Mrs. Garth's tent. Garnett and Pruitt found a place near Marshal Fargo, Lowry and the other two men from town. It was a miserable night. The mosquitoes came up out of the grass by the stream in swarms. The chill in the air didn't seem to bother the insects. Nobody got much sleep. Finally, at the first sign of dawn, the insects disappeared.

Lowry made the fire again. They had a quick meal of beef jerky, biscuits with apple jelly and coffee, then rode on. By noon they came to a small mining town with a beanery. The posse had a dinner of venison steak, baked yams, and pole beans. After that, they had apple pie and coffee. Lowry picked up a small smoked ham and three dozen eggs, which he put carefully on the packhorse. They rode on and the next morning he found all the eggs broken. He served everyone scrambled eggs and ham.

Over the next three days they fell into a routine. One morning, just as they were getting into the rhythm of things, it started to rain. It came down hard for hours and they rode along slumped over their saddles. Pruitt was the only one caught without a slicker. He was quickly soaked to the bone. The coach road became muddy and the horses had trouble walking. Finally, they were forced to ride alongside the road through the tall bunch grass that slowed them down even more. It rained for five hours then suddenly stopped.

Just before dark, they came to a small place called Johnson's Slough alongside the trail. It was a collection of sod huts with a saloon, a beanery, and a bawdy house. It seemed odd that it was even there. They later learned the stream that ran behind the place once had gold. It ran out after two years, and most of the prospectors packed up and left. The beanery, saloon, and bawdy house stayed on to serve travelers, drifters, and outlaws.

Two of the men from Easton's Corners headed for the bawdy house. Sloan Braddock, Warfield, Wheeler, Preston and Pete Lowry went into the saloon. Young Pruitt walked in behind them. Marshal Fargo, Mrs. Garth and Garnett headed for the beanery.

It wasn't very clean, but they were hungry and the aroma of garlic and onions was enough to make their mouths water. They sat around a worn, splintering wooden table that had a sputtering oil lamp on it. The lamp's chimney was covered with dark soot and the walls of the place, being built of sod, had a damp, earthy smell. A damp draft came up from the dirt floor. A moth flew back and forth over the oil lamp.

A small, middle aged woman dressed in a soiled, worn, brown cotton dress and filthy white apron, came from the back. Her hair was straggly and hung over her forehead and large, dark eyes. She gave them an odd look. Garnett couldn't figure out if she was afraid, surprised or both. She quickly got some spoons, forks, and knives from under the counter and put them on the table. Her hands shook. She seemed edgy, almost frightened.

"All we have is beef stew an' sourdough biscuits with lard," the woman muttered in a low voice.

The marshal nodded and said, "Sure, thet's fine, ma'am."

The woman left and came back five minutes later with a pile of biscuits, a plate with salted lard, and three bowls of steaming stew on a tray. After she served it, she walked over to the counter, sat on a stool and waited. She often glanced at them as they ate, but mostly she kept her eyes on the door. Seeing how nervous the woman was, Garnett glanced at the marshal to see if he noticed. It seemed like he didn't. His attention was on his bowl of stew.

They ate in silence. The stew was a bit salty, but other than that it was good. It had large chunks of meat, plenty of carrots, and turnips. Big chunks of garlic floated in the gravy. They were hungry and ate quickly. The woman kept glancing nervously at the door. When they had finished eating, she quickly walked over to their table.

"Finished?" she asked, as if in a hurry to see them go.

"How about pie and coffee?" the marshal asked.

"Alright," she said grudgingly, as she quickly cleared the table and scurried off into the kitchen.

As she rushed away, Garnett remarked, "She seems in a hurry to get rid of us."

The marshal replied, "I hadn't noticed." He rubbed his belly. "That sure was fine stew."

In a few minutes, they were eating apple pie and drinking coffee. When they were done, they sat back feeling satisfied. The women cleared the table. When she returned, she told them it was six bits total. Garnett paid.

The marshal asked Sandra, "Mind if I smoke, ma'am?"

"No, go right ahead, Marshal."

Marshal Fargo pulled the makings from his vest pocket and began to roll a cigarette. Garnett did the same. Mrs. Garth watched Garnett as he worked the paper and tobacco. "Where are you from, Mr. Garnett?" she asked. Garnett chuckled. "Did I say something amusing, Mr. Garnett?"

"It's not you, ma'am, it's me. I always have trouble with that question. I got out of prison a while ago."

"Did you say prison?"

"I must confess, I did say prison, ma'am, ashamed as I am to admit it."

"Did you murder someone?"

"No, ma'am, I robbed a bank."

"A bank? Just one?"

"Yup, just one, ma'am. I was doing good until my horse tossed me and the posse picked me up off the road."

"Well, that was very nice of them, wasn't it?"

"Oh, yeah, real nice. The judge was even nicer. He gave me seven years in Storeyville Prison."

"Seven years? That's pretty harsh."

"They let me out in four years, so it wasn't all that bad."

The marshal looked at Garnett. "I'm gonna retire soon. I kin put in a good word fer you, Garnett, if yer interested."

Garnett smiled. "I'll sleep on it, Marshal."

"You do that, Garnett. I'm serious."

The sound of rushing footsteps came from outside. They stopped at the door. A bearded, grizzly face appeared in the window and then quickly pulled back out of sight. The woman saw the face, too, and looked frightened. She stared over at the table and blurted out, "Don't go outside, they're waitin' ta ambush ya!"

They heard gunfire. It seemed to come from the saloon, up the road. The marshal, Mrs. Garth and Garnett stood up, staring at the front door.

"Come with me," the woman said. "Y'all kin sneak out the back and hide!"

Garnett glanced at the marshal. "Take Mrs. Garth."

"You sure?"

"Yeah. Get going!"

The marshal and Mrs. Garth followed the woman into the kitchen. Garnett stood poised, staring at the door latch, waiting for it to move. It gave a twitch and the door flew open. Two big, husky men burst into the room. One had a shotgun and the other had an old pistol.

Garnett flipped the table up and dropped down behind it just as the shotgun went off. He felt the impact of the lead buckshot as it slammed against the wood. Splinters flew everywhere. The lamp that had been on the table shattered on the sod floor. It went out as the oil soaked into the dirt, casting the room in darkness.

The man with the gun fired several shots at the table. The bullets passed through, narrowly missing Garnett's shoulder. Then he heard the hammer falling on an empty cylinder.

Garnett quickly stood up. The light from the kitchen showed the two attackers were still standing in the doorway, twenty feet away. Garnett fanned off two quick shots into each man's chest. They grunted and moved towards him. He fanned off two more shots. This time the force of the bullets slammed them back out onto the street. They fell flat and didn't move.

More gunfire could be heard in the distance. Garnett ran outside, jumped over the two bodies and headed for the saloon, reloading his gun. When he got there, it was pitch black inside except for the flash of guns. The fight went on for a few seconds more, and then stopped.

Garnett waited a minute before yelling, "Anybody alive in there?"

"That you, Garnett?" Rick Pruitt yelled back.

"Yeah! You okay, kid?"

"Yeah! Come on in!"

Garnett walked in with his gun drawn. He saw a man behind the bar lighting a lamp. He looked pale and shaken.

The place was a mess. Tables were overturned and chairs were scattered everywhere. Bodies lay on the floor while others were draped over tables and chairs. In all, Garnett counted eight of them.

Braddock and Warfield stood in the center of the open area by the bar, reloading their guns. Wheeler, Preston and Pete Lowry lay badly shot up on the floor near the bar, all three dead.

"Jesus!" Garnett said.

Braddock turned to Garnett. "Where's Mrs. Garth? Is she okay?"

"Yeah, she's with Marshal Fargo."

"What about the other two men from town?" Pruitt asked.

"They went down to the bawdy house," Braddock said. "What about them?"

"They must have heard all the shooting. How come they didn't show up ta help us?"

Warfield said, "Yeah, that's funny ain't it? I'll go check on 'em."

He left and the marshal and Mrs. Garth came walking into the saloon. She saw the bodies and gasped.

"Maybe you should wait outside, Sandra," Braddock said.

"No, I'm fine," she replied.

The marshal looked at the barman. "You know them?"

"Nope. They came in early today and hung around. I got no idea who they are. There's two more, somewhere."

"Not anymore," Garnett said. "They're layin' dead in the road, down by the beanery."

The barman looked worried. "What about the woman? Is she alright? She's my mom."

"She's fine," the marshal replied. "Thanks to her, Mrs. Garth an' me got away."

The barman sighed in relief, put up some shot glasses and poured whiskey. "On the house," he said.

Everyone went to the bar, grabbed a shot and tossed it down. The barman refilled the glasses. This time they drank slower, waiting for Warfield.

It wasn't long before he returned alone. He shook his head. "All two are dead. Shot in the back. Their guns and gunbelts are gone, and it looks like they were robbed."

"What about the girls? There are four of them and the whoremonger," the barman said.

"They're gone. The place is empty as an egg shell," Warfield replied.

The barman nodded. "They must have cut out in his covered wagon. They live out of it. But you'll never find 'em in the dark. No tellin' which way they went."

"Gosh," Pruitt said. "What a lousy way ta croak!"

Warfield nodded. "Yeah, they probably never saw it comin'."

Mrs. Garth turned to Marshal Fargo. "Marshal, your three men from town are dead. Why don't you take their bodies back home? You're out of your jurisdiction now, anyway, aren't you?"

The old lawman scratched his chin and gave that some serious thought. "We're too far from Easton's Corners now, ma'am. They'd be ripe by the time I got halfway back. It'll be better if I give 'em a decent burial here an' go find yer little girl. Thet's what they'd want me ta do anyway."

Sandra put a sympathetic hand on the marshal's arm. "Of course, Marshal. You're right."

The marshal looked around. The group had started out with eleven people. They had lost five men in a matter of minutes. Now it was just himself, Garnett, Pruitt, Braddock, Warfield and Mrs. Garth.

"We walked right into this one," the marshal said sadly, shaking his head. "Damn it! I shoulda been more careful!"

Garnett said, "You're not to blame, Marshal."

"Yeah," Pruitt said. "You had no way of knowing. None of us did."

Marshal Fargo glared at the barman. "No, we had no way of knowing, but you sure as hell did, didn't you, mister?"

The barman cringed under the marshal's accusing stare. "Yeah, I knew, but they had a gun on me. What could I do, Marshal?"

The marshal softened. "Yeah, I guess I would a-done the same thing." He paused a moment. "Any idea who they were?"

The barman shrugged. "Just drifters and no accounts. Robbers, thieves, and murderers, I reckon. We git 'em all the time. They just drift in here an' roost, like a cat waitin' fer a bird."

"Then I guess we did you a favor, didn't we?" Braddock observed.

The barman shrugged. "Yeah, but y'all shot the hell outta my bar. Who's gonna pay fer that?"

"I sure as hell ain't," Warfield shot back.

"Me, neither!" Pruitt said emphatically.

Braddock suggested, "He can take the dead men's horses, Marshal. He can sell them and the saddles and gear."

"Horses? Them varmints didn't have no horses. They was after yer horses and everythin' else ya got," the barman complained.

The marshal considered this for a moment then turned to Braddock. "How about givin' him Wheeler's and Preston's horses and guns, seein' as they're dead and don't need 'em?"

"Sure, I guess," Braddock replied solemnly.

"We'll keep the three horses and guns that belonged to Pete Lowry and the other two men from town," Marshal Fargo said. "We'll leave them here and pick them up on the way back. I'll give 'em back to their families."

"That would be the right thing to do," Sandra Garth said. "Thet makes good sense."

The marshal turned to the barman. "Is thet okay? You'll git near eight hundred dollars fer them two horses an' the saddles an' tack on 'em. Maybe more."

"Sure, I guess that'd be okay," the barman replied. "But what about the bodies? You gonna jest leave 'em there?"

"You got any ideas?" the marshal asked.

"We kin toss them in the stream. They'll be miles away by mornin'," Warfield said.

"No, we'd best burn them," the marshal said. "It's the best way."

Garnett and Pruitt went about stripping the dead of their guns and gunbelts, and gave everything to the barman. The marshal had the bodies hauled out back by the stream and dumped in a pile. He poured lamp oil over them and set them afire. They all stood watching until the heat and smell of burning flesh drove them back into the bar.

"Ma'am, you can sleep in the back room, if you want to," the barman said after they'd had another drink. "There's a cot back there and a water basin and all."

"Thank you," Sandra replied. She said goodnight to the others and walked to the back of the saloon.

After she left, the barman added, "You men can sleep on the tables and chairs, whatever suits you."

"Come on, boys," the marshal said to the rest. "We gotta bury Lowry and the boys from town."

By the time they were finished, they were exhausted and emotionally drained. They got their bedrolls and made the best of it sleeping on chairs, across tables, and atop the bar. As tired as they were, the stink of blood and stale air kept them awake for hours. They got little sleep and morning came much too slowly. When it finally arrived, daylight and the rising sun was a welcome sight. They walked outside and inhaled the sweet freshness of a new day. The crisp air stimulated them and made them realize how hungry they were. After a full breakfast at the beanery, they went on their way.

Chapter 6

There were only six of them left now. Marshal Fargo and Jesse Garnett took the lead while Rick Pruitt and Warfield rode in the rear, keeping an eye on the packhorse. Braddock and Sandra Garth rode in the center, close together, talking. Sometimes she broke out laughing at something he said, unheard by the others.

Last night had been a miserable one. The men had slept wrapped in their blankets on chairs and tables. The stench of the sawdust covered floor smelled like stale tobacco juice, rotgut, and blood. Yet, it was better than sleeping outside on the damp, flea infested ground.

Mrs. Garth fared better in the little room in the back, but she would never forget the sickening stench of burning flesh. It penetrated everything and clung to hair and clothing. The smell upset the horses, too, making them restless all night. The coming of dawn felt like a blessing.

Riding all that day, they stopped twice briefly to eat and rest the horses. At sundown, they found a small stream with grass along its banks in a grove of silver aspens. They made camp, had a quick meal of biscuits and jerky, then turned in for the night. They slept the sleep of the dead, ignoring the mosquitoes and the damp cold that rose from the ground.

The next day it rained on and off until noon and then the sun came out. It got hot again and they suffered until the old coach road went through a large stand of pine trees where it was cooler in the shadows. On the other side of the pines, the trail led up a long hill.

They stopped at the top to look down at a fast running stream that stretched for miles in both directions. A raft built of logs swayed in the current at the water's edge. It was attached to a crossing line on the near side of the stream. A man sat on a boulder by the edge of the stream reading a magazine and waiting for a customer to come.

"Whatta you think?" Garnett asked the marshal.

"It's the only way across," Marshal Fargo replied.

"It looks fishy ta me," Pruitt said.

"Fishy? How so?" Warfield asked.

"I don't know. It jest looks fishy, is all."

The marshal smirked. "Christ, kid, you see a spook behind every rock. You're a regular worrywart."

"We got no choice. Let's go," Braddock said. Sandra nodded in approval.

The gambler led the way down the slope, across a field of whiskey grass and up to the landing. A sign nailed to a tree demanded an eagle for each person and animal. The bargeman was a big, beefy bruiser the size of a grizzly bear. Scraggly hair hung down his hatless head, almost covering his eyes. He wore overalls but no shoes, shirt or hat.

The marshal approached him. "Yer price is kinda steep, ain't it, mister?"

The bargeman gave the marshal a smirk. "Well, you can always walk across, Marshal. Or swim, if ya care to."

The marshal took up a collection and handed the bargeman the money for the six people and the horses. The bargeman dropped it into a can nailed to a nearby tree.

"Three at a time," the bargeman said as he grabbed a long pole and stepped onto the barge.

Braddock, Sandra Garth and Warfield walked their horses onto the barge and waited as the bargeman untied the securing rope and began poling the barge to the other side. The two guide ropes looped around the crossing line high above them kept the barge from being swept downstream. The push of the current against the side of the barge helped it move along.

It was slow going at first, but once in the middle of the stream they gained speed. In twenty minutes they landed safely on the far side. Getting off, they walked their horses up the grassy slope to level ground and waited for the others. The bargeman pushed the barge back to the other side to get the marshal, Garnett and Pruitt. With no load to hold it down, the barge literally shot back across the stream in minutes.

"You and Garnett go on," Pruitt said. "I'll stay with the packhorse."

"Don't worry about thet horse, sonny," the bargeman said. "I'll see it gits over okay. I'll tie him on nice so he can't go nowhere."

"Yeah, well, I'd feel better if I stayed with him," the young cowboy insisted.

The marshal scowled. "Stop yer jabberin' an' git on the barge, kid. We ain't got all day."

Pruitt shrugged and walked his horse onto the barge. The bargeman grabbed his pole and shoved off. The current caught the barge and they gained speed. Garnett, Pruitt and the marshal were soon on the other side and up on top of the slope with Braddock, Warfield and Sandra Garth. They all watched as the barge made its way to the far side.

Once there, the bargeman tied the barge fast, walked over to a boulder, sat there, and rolled a cigarette.

"What the heck is he up to?" Warfield asked.

"He's taking a rest, I suppose," Sandra replied.

They waited and watched. When the bargeman was finished smoking, he walked behind the boulder out of sight. Moments later they saw a rifle barrel appear along the left side of it. There was a puff of smoke and then a gun's bark. A second later, a bullet hit Warfield in the chest. He fell forward and rolled down the hill, into the water. It quickly carried his body downstream, bobbing and turning until it was finally out of sight.

"Get back!" Braddock yelled. They grabbed the reins and quickly pulled their horses behind a high berm.

"Kid," the marshal said, "the next time I argue with you, slap me! You were plumb right about this guy."

"Thet's okay, Marshal," Pruitt said, "yer young yet. You'll learn as ya git older." The marshal scowled at him. He didn't like being lectured to by a whippersnapper.

"What are we going to do now, Sloan?" Sandra Garth asked Braddock, as if he had the answer.

"I guess we'll have to give up on the packhorse, Sandra," the gambler replied.

No one offered a better idea until Garnett said, "Kid, can you swim?"

Pruitt said, "Nope."

"Then I guess I'll have to do it myself."

"Do what?" Sandra asked.

"Go over there and get the packhorse, ma'am."

Garnett began removing his gunbelt and clothes. When he had nothing on but his Levi's, he stopped.

"You all lean over the top of the berm and start firing back at him every few minutes, just to keep him busy dodging bullets," Garnett said.

"Be careful, Mr. Garnett!" Sandra Garth warned.

"I'll sure try, ma'am."

Without another word, Garnett crouched low and ran along the berm, following it downward. The bark of guns echoed behind him. Stopping a moment to listen, he slid down a grassy slope on his backside until he hit the rocky beach.

Once there, he looked around and took stock of his situation. He was now a good hundred yards upstream of the barge and could see the bargeman where he stood firing across at the others from behind the boulder. Every few seconds he would jerk back as a bullet came his way from the other side. They were doing a good job keeping him occupied.

Garnett walked down to the stream and eased his body into the water. It was cold and for a moment, it took his breath away. He began swimming against the swift current, paddling hard as it carried him downstream toward the barge.

It was slow going and took a full fifteen minutes to get to the other side. He was only about thirty feet upstream from the boulder.

Hiding behind a bush, Garnett waited until he caught his breath. His heart was pounding and it took a while to calm down. Once he felt ready, Garnett picked up a rock and rushed toward the boulder. The others saw him and stopped shooting. The bargeman saw his chance and started firing back at them.

He never suspected someone was rushing up behind him. Garnett swung the rock hard against the back of his head. There was a dull crunching sound. The bargeman dropped his rifle and slumped sideways with a long sigh. Garnett stared down at him to make sure he was dead. Satisfied, he dropped the rock and rolled the body over.

Going through the bargeman's pockets for matches and the makings, Garnett leaned against the boulder, rolled a cigarette and lit it. Across the stream, the others were cheering and waving at him. He waved wearily back. When he felt rested enough to go on, Garnett took the money out of the can nailed to the tree and put it in a saddlebag of the packhorse. Minutes later, he had the animal tied on and was poling the barge to the other side.

It took Garnett a little longer to get across than it did the bargeman, but he finally made it.

Chapter 7

Two days later, late in the afternoon, they rode, dusty and exhausted, into the mining town of Coldwater Springs. Like most mining towns, it had a bathhouse, several saloons, gambling halls, a hotel, a flophouse and all the other trappings of a large, thriving gold mining town. The amount of luxury one enjoyed in Coldwater Springs depended on how much money one had. Braddock and Sandra Garth took rooms on the second floor of the expensive Queen's Hotel, which had its own upscale restaurant.

"Would you take our horses down to the stables and have them attended to, Marshal Fargo?" Mrs. Garth asked. It sounded more like an order than a request.

"Sure, ma'am," the marshal replied, "I'd be glad to." As they headed for the stables, the old lawman took off his badge and stuck it in his vest pocket.

Garnett noticed and said, "Smart move."

"It's worthless here, anyway," the marshal said. "No sense attractin' attention."

They left all the horses at the stables for an overnight stay. "They'll need the works, sonny," the marshal told the stable hand. "Treat 'em good or I'll kick yer skinny little butt."

"Six bits each," the young man said, not at all fazed by the threat. Garnett paid from the bargeman's kitty.

Leaving their horses at the stables, they headed across town to the London House, a fancy name for a flea parlor that served as a hotel for cowboys and prospectors. They took one room with two cots and flipped a coin to see who slept on the floor. Young Pruitt lost. The mattresses were stuffed with horsehair and, in themselves, were hotels for bedbugs and lice. The weary travelers dropped their saddlebags and bedrolls, locked the room door and then went looking for a place to eat.

"You know," Pruitt remarked as they walked along the plank sidewalk to avoid the muddy road, "I don't trust thet Braddock fellah."

"Here we go agin," the marshal said. "Kid, yer the most suspicious minded person I ever met and thet's fer sure."

"No, I mean it. He wants that thousand dollar reward so bad he kin taste it."

"As fer as I'm concerned, he kin have it," the marshal replied. "I don't git a penny exceptin' what my job pays."

Pruitt shrugged. "Then, as it stands, it gits split between me, Garnett here, an' Braddock."

"Yeah, if'n we find the girl. We don't know fer sure where she is or if she's alive."

Garnett said, "I know how to find out, Marshal."

"Yeah? How's thet?"

"Talk to a barman. Barmen get to hear things we don't get to hear."

"Yer right there, Garnett," the marshal said. "Sooner or later somebody spills the beans to a barman. Especially when they've had one drink too many."

"There's three saloons in town," Garnett said. "Let's split up. Each of us take one."

"Let's eat first," Pruitt replied. "I'm hungry."

The marshal nodded. "I'm all fer thet, kid."

They found a beanery nearby, ate a hearty meal and left. "We'll meet back here at the beanery," the marshal said.

They split up and went in different directions. Garnett walked into the Lucky Nugget Saloon. The room was filled with cowboys, prospectors, card sharks and townsfolk. He sidled up to the bar, ordered a whiskey and waited for a chance to engage the barman in idle talk. It finally came.

"Maybe you know of some fellahs passing through who had a young girl with them. She was dressed pretty fancy."

"Yeah, they were here for a short spell. The girl didn't seem too happy."

"You don't happen to know where they went, do you?"

"No, but you might try Karren's place."

"Karren's place?"

"Yeah, it's a swanky gambling hall, further down."

Garnett finished his drink and left. He could see the place, several buildings down, on the other side of the road. It had a large sign over its doors that read Karren's House of Chance.

He headed in that direction and in two minutes was inside looking around. It was brightly lit with poker tables, black jack, baccarat, and wheels of chance. Men with rifles sat on pedestals in each corner, watching the crowd. Guards walked amongst the customers, looking for signs of trouble. The place was packed with gamblers of every sort, from amateurs to professionals. Garnett noticed some of them carried small sacks of gold nuggets that they exchanged for gambling chits.

It took a while to find the woman named Karren. She was a pretty woman with short brown hair, deep blue eyes and a sulking, sensual, I don't give a damn smile. Her earrings would have cost a cowboy ten years' wages and her dress even more. She looked Garnett over approvingly and nodded. As she moved in closer, he got a good whiff of her expensive perfume.

"Hi, handsome, what can I do for you? Something, I hope," Karren said, looking the six foot-two, broad shouldered ex-outlaw up and down. From the smile on her lips, it was clear she liked what she saw.

"I'm looking for some men with a young girl," Garnett said, also liking what he saw. Her mouth was inviting and he found it hard not to stare at it.

"Three men and a girl? Yeah, they were here," Karren replied. "The girl look spooked. When she tried to talk to me, they shut her up real fast. Is she kin?"

"Of a friend, yes. She's been kidnapped. You don't happen you know if they're still in town, do you?"

"Well, they haven't been around since they lost big at the wheels and tables, a few days ago. I'd say they left."

"Thank you, ma'am."

As Garnett turned to walk away, Karren asked, "What's your name, handsome?"

"Garnett. Jesse Garnett, ma'am."

Karren put a hand on his arm. "What's your hurry? Stick around. Maybe we can get to know each other better."

"Oh, I'd like to, ma'am, I really would. But I can't. Not right now. Maybe later?"

"I don't believe in later. It's a onetime offer, handsome. It's now or never. Take it or leave it."

"I'm hating myself already, ma'am," Garnett said regretfully. "I really am. It's the best offer I've ever had." He saluted the lady and hurried off. He could hear her laughing behind him as he left.

He found Marshal Fargo and Pruitt inside the beanery. He told them what he had learned.

"They're most likely heading towards Cheyenne Wells, to thet robber's roost I told you all about, the Snake Pit," the marshal said.

"How come you know so much about thet Snake Pit place, Marshal?" Pruitt asked.

"Because I was there once, sonny, when I was a bounty hunter. I know every outlaw hideaway this side of the Colorado Mountains. Does thet answer yer question?"

"It sure does, Marshal," Pruitt conceded. "But how do you know they took her there?"

The marshal scratched his stubbly chin. "Wal, I don't know fer sure, but thet's where I'd be a-headin' if a posse was a-ridin' up my backside. I'd hide there a day or two or three, an' then head south fer the Texas panhandle."

"How far is it to thet place a yers, Marshal?" Pruitt asked.

"Oh, maybe a day's ride or more. Ain't all thet far."

They went to the Thirsty Bull Saloon, had two drinks, then back to their room in the flophouse. It was dark and they welcomed a chance to rest after a long day on the trail. The marshal and Garnett lay on their cots smoking while Pruitt lay on his bedroll on the floor deep in thought.

"I wonder what she looks like?" Pruitt asked.

"Who?" the marshal asked.

"The girl. Mrs. Garth's daughter. I wonder if she's as pretty as her mom."

The old marshal laughed. "She might be and she might not be. Jest because her mom is pretty don't mean she's gonna be pretty. I saw situations where the mom is ugly as sin and the daughter as pretty as a picture. Ya jest never know."

Garnett snickered. "I wouldn't dwell on it, kid."

"Why not?" Pruitt asked.

"Because she's way out of yer class. Her mom won't let you lay an eye or a finger on her," Garnett replied.

The marshal snickered and said, "You got thet right, Garnett."

Pruitt sighed. "Yeah, I guess yer right about thet, alright."

"Go to sleep, kid," the marshal said. "Maybe you'll dream yer married to her."

They all laughed, then fell quiet. Later, a drunken cowboy in the next room began to snore. He sounded like a constipated bull.

Chapter 8

The Snake Pit was a small collection of pinewood shacks and sod huts located southwest of Sharon Springs, in the Kansas badlands. It was a sanctuary for bank robbers, train robbers, murderers, and other lawbreakers. Some stayed there permanently and some rode south to the Texas panhandle, further on across the border into New Mexico or further south into Juarez. It was one of many such places located throughout the West that accommodated outlaws, if they knew where to find them. And most did.

Situated east of the Colorado line and nestled between two high mountain ranges, the Snake Pit was an ideal robber's roost. Built on the site of a dead silver mine, the Snake Pit once had a stage stop located in its midst. It was an ideal place for a town because a wide stream ran pure and free nearby.

The largest and most important building in the Snake Pit was the Crown Jewel Hotel, Bar, Beanery, and Mercantile. It was owned, and operated by retired outlaw Desmond Ferris. The building was unique in that it was a two floor, pine log structure with wings. As customers entered the lobby in front, a sign directed them to the mercantile in the rear. A set of stairs along one wall, by the lobby desk, led to the upper floor where Ferris rented out rooms. As visitors entered the lobby from the street, they had the choice of turning left into a beanery, or right into a saloon. Ferris had thought of everything.

When Kinsey Blue, Wade Downy, Sam Meany and Hugh Mason rode in with young Lacey Garth, they took two rooms up on the second floor. Downy, Meany and Mason stayed in one room while Blue took a room for himself and the girl. When Ferris saw the sad condition the girl was in, he became very nervous. Her hands were tied together. She looked pale and weak. Ferris hoped their stay wouldn't be long.

Blue saw the look on Ferris' face. "She's a runaway. We're takin' her back ta her pappy fer the reward," he said with a crooked smile.

Ferris knew that was an outright lie. The look in the girl's frightened eyes told as much. She was too scared to say a word. "Where's Ram Harper?" Ferris asked. He and Harper had ridden the outlaw trail together.

"We had a difference of opinion," Blue said. "I won."

Ferris didn't ask any more questions. He knew of Blue's reputation as a loose cannon.

Later, in their room, Downy, Meany and Mason discussed their situation. They were bothered by Blue taking the girl and shooting Ram Harper in the back. Besides that, there was the large amount of money Blue had lost in the gambling halls in Coldwater Springs. Also, heavy on their minds was the fact that Blue had made himself boss without asking any of them.

But the taking of the girl was what bothered them the most. She had not only slowed them down, but had put them in a bad situation. This was not a bar girl or a painted lady. She had class. If the law caught up with them, they would be hung on the spot without a trial. Prison was temporary, but hanging was permanent. Once they hung you that was the end of red eye and painted ladies. No more riding tall in the saddle, feeling the wind in your face and hearing the posse's bullets snapping. No, the taking of the girl was a bad move, and Downy, Mason and Meany didn't like it at all.

"You know what I'm a-thinkin'?" Mason said. "I'm thinkin' Blue ain't gonna ask fer no ransom at all. I think he's taken an interest in the girl. He's up to somethin' an' it don't include us."

Downy nodded. "Yeah, that could be. It does seem like he's got somethin' up his sleeve."

"I'd jest as soon cut her loose," Meany said. "She's been a pain in the neck all the way."

"Best kill her out in the woods and leave her body fer the coyotes," Mason suggested. "Kill her an' be done with it."

"Kill her? Why kill her?" Downy asked.

"It's the only way ta git Blue's head straightened out," Mason replied.

Meany got a bottle of whiskey from his saddlebag, took a pull and passed it around. "How long are we gonna stay in this hole?" he asked.

"Heck if I know," Mason replied.

"Well," Downy said, "the way Blue is spendin' the money, we're gonna have ta rob another bank real soon, an' thet's fer sure."

75

"Yeah, an' it ain't right thet he won't split the money with us," Meany replied. "It ain't right."

They went quiet again. Blue had them scared. He was crazy and unpredictable. They felt as trapped as the girl was, in many ways.

Downy looked around. "This damn fleabag of a room reminds me of a prison cell," he said. "It's startin' ta stink, too." It was a cramped room with a cot and a double bunk.

"I sure hope we head fer Texas real soon," Mason grumbled.

As for Blue, he had a large room with two beds. His plan was to have the girl and himself sleep with their clothes on. At night, he made her take her boots off and tied a rope hobble to her ankle and his. He also locked the door so that if she did slip the hobble she still couldn't get away. If she needed to wash up, he would leave the room, lock the door and wait in the hall.

Blue had it all figured out. During the day, the girl would wear a hobble. In the large crowds, no one would notice or even care. She was just another girl in the Snake Pit. How or why was nobody's business. He had Downy,

Mason and Meany stay close to her, in case she bolted and went for the law.

The one thing Blue's mind couldn't figure out was how to get the girl to like him. She was so intelligent it scared him. In addition to that, she was beautiful. He didn't want to hurt her. The fact was, of late, she had been getting the best of him and he rather liked it. It was sort of fun, like a game. He wanted to keep her around forever. Someday, she would come to like him. He was sure of that.

They were in the Snake Pit longer than planned because Blue's gambling suddenly turned for the better. He started winning big and got irritated when Mason or Downy tried to talk him into riding out for Texas.

Lacey Garth had one thought that kept hope alive. She knew her mother would never rest until she found her, and she knew a posse was on the road searching for her this very minute. Old Marshal Fargo had been a good friend to the Garth family. He would never let her down.

But after a week at the Snake Pit, her faith began to weaken. Maybe they had given up the search. Anyway, the marshal probably wouldn't come this far out of his jurisdiction to find her. He had no power out here in this land of cutthroats and criminals. The few good people who lived in the Snake Pit had no authority. There was no law there. There was not even a jail or marshal. The gun, the knife and money ruled.

One day Lacey heard them talking. Blue was thinking of heading for the Texas panhandle. She knew that would be the end of life as she knew it and thought about killing herself. Better to die than to live like this. The next time she was left alone in the room she would throw herself out of the window. If she was lucky, she would break her neck.

Anything was better than this.

Chapter 9

"Maybe it would be best if you stayed here at the hotel, Mrs. Garth," the marshal said. They were outside the Queen's Hotel in Coldwater Springs. It was morning and the sky was cloudy. It would be a good day to travel. "Things might git rough when we reach the Snake Pit. We'll git in there an' out as quickly as we can."

"No, Marshal," Sandra Garth replied. "I can't. The waiting is too hard."

The old lawman nodded. He understood. "Alright. It's yer call, ma'am."

Sloan Braddock cut in. "I'll keep an eye on her, Marshal Fargo. She'll be just fine."

The marshal gave Braddock a look cold as steel. "You be sure ta do thet, Braddock."

They mounted up and left Coldwater Springs. It started to rain again. They put on their slickers, except for Pruitt. He still had none. Marshal Fargo took the lead, while Pruitt came behind with the packhorse. Garnett fell back alongside him.

"You look like a wet hen, Pruitt."

"Ta heck with you, Garnett."

Garnett chuckled and rode ahead, passing Braddock and Sandra Garth. He stopped alongside the marshal.

"This is good," Garnett said, "they'll most likely stay put wherever they are if it keeps raining."

"I hope you're right about thet," the marshal replied.

Garnett didn't say anything more. He rode relaxed in the saddle, sometimes glancing around into the woods. He began to wonder why he was there in the first place. Was it for the money, or was it to help a woman who feared for her only child? He could only imagine the pain she was suffering.

Garnett glanced back at Sandra and Braddock, twenty feet behind. They rode close, talking. Sometimes Braddock laughed. Sandra nodded often, smiled and put a hand on his arm as they rode along. It was as if they were old friends. More than that, it gave the impression they were man and wife, or lovers. Garnett knew Braddock had a nose for money, and Sandra Garth, being the wife of a cattle rancher, was worth plenty.

It stopped raining. They stopped long enough to remove their slickers then rode on. An hour later they saw motion up ahead. Seven armed men had emerged from the trees and were walking in their direction. When they saw Marshal Fargo and Garnett, they spread out and blocked the road. They wore gunbelts and guns. The guns were already out and aimed.

Braddock was quick to act. He brought his horse up alongside the marshal. Pruitt came up on the outside next to Garnett.

"Stay back behind us, Mrs. Garth," the marshal said loudly.

"Alright!"

Sandra Garth walked her horse backwards twenty feet and stopped, leaving some space between her and the others.

The man in the middle seemed to be the leader. He was taller than the rest, had a full beard and wore a Union coat with a junior officer's insignia on the collar. The other men also wore signs of once being in the Union army, hats, coats, or pants of blue.

"Yer blockin' the road," the marshal said. "How about lettin' us pass?"

"Sure, you can pass, old man," the officer said. "Just leave your money, guns, and horses here and go on about your business." By the way the man talked, it was plain he was well educated.

"Why should we do that, Lieutenant?" Garnett asked.

"Because it's the only way you'll get to stay alive this day, my friend."

Garnett's big appaloosa sensed the tension. It snorted and shifted nervously.

"Is that the game?" Marshal Fargo asked.

"I'm afraid so, my friend," the officer answered calmly.

"Well, I sure don't like it, mister. Yer a disgrace to the army."

The officer smiled. "My friends and I left the army a long time ago, old man. It didn't have much to offer." The others chuckled and nodded, as if proud of what they had done.

"So, yer a bunch a deserters, are ya?"

"Not to change the subject, old man, but you and your friend have three seconds to get down off your horses and start walking."

For an answer, Marshal Fargo yelled in anger, "Draw, ya yellah dogs!"

The marshal, Braddock, Garnett and Pruitt drew and fanned off one shot each, catching the outlaws by surprise. Their shots were true and left four of them dead on the road. The officer, unhurt, drew and fired at the marshal but missed when the lawman's horse shifted on him. Garnett saw it and fanned of a shot at the officer, hitting him in the chest, knocking him backwards onto the road. He hit the ground hard and lay there. The two other outlaws still alive threw up their hands.

"I had enough!" one yelled. "Don't kill me!"

The marshal growled, "Alright then, drop yer guns." The two men tossed their guns on the road. "We're movin' on, so git off the road. If you follow us, we'll kill ya both. Then we'll find yer mommy an' daddy an' kill them as well. If they got a dog, we'll kill it, too. You git my drift?"

"Yes, sir," one of them replied. He was badly shaken.

"Let's ride," the marshal said to Garnett and the others. They struck out down the road at a fast canter. When they were a mile further on they stopped, looked back and waited to see if they were being followed.

"I think they got the message, Marshal," Braddock said.

"Everybody alright?" Marshal Fargo asked. They all nodded. "Darn it all," the marshal said sadly. "What a waste."

"You had no choice, Marshal Fargo," Sandra Garth said. "They wouldn't listen. You tried to reason with them, but they had their minds set."

Pruitt looked sad. "Those darn fools." He reloaded and the others did the same.

"Let's keep movin'," Garnett said.

They rode on. Time dragged. It rained off and on. Toward evening, they stopped to camp by a stream that ran through a stand of pines. They built a fire to dry out. Humans and horses were hungry and exhausted.

It rained again during the night. They spent long, miserable hours huddled together. When the sun finally came up, Sandra found some wild strawberries, and they ate them along with jerky and hardtack. They got a fire going and she made coffee. The hot, black liquid shocked them awake like the kick of a mule. It started to rain again as they broke camp and rode on once more.

Around noon the rain stopped, and they found shelter under some pine trees by a clear stream. The horses drank and ate grass while the humans ate beef jerky and hardtack, cursing each bite.

Braddock produced a flask. "Brandy, Sandra? For the chill?"

She nodded and took a short drink. "That was good. Thank you, Sloan." They were now casually calling each other by their first names. It was as if they had known each other for years.

Pruitt leaned close to Garnett and whispered, "Well, now, look at thet. What do we have here? It looks like two love birds ta me." Garnett smiled and nodded.

Braddock put his flask away and looked at the marshal. "How far now, Marshal?"

The marshal gave that some thought. "Well, now, let me see. Sharon Springs is about five miles west from where we are now. When we get there, we turn south an' ride a good fifteen miles more."

They built another fire to dry out. Later, they got going. After an hour, they reached the outskirts of Sharon Springs. It was a big, bustling place with heavy traffic going in and out of the city. They left the horses to be fed, watered, and brushed downed at the stables near the edge of town. At a nearby beanery, they ate a full meal of steak, fried onions, and sweet potatoes, topping it off with apple pie and coffee. Feeling much revived, they mounted up again, and started out on the last leg of their journey. By late afternoon they rode into the back end of a place called the Snake Pit.

A stable was located at the edge of town. They dismounted and waited as the marshal asked the owner some questions. While he was doing that, Mrs. Garth walked among the stalls. She saw several horses tied up separately in a large stall and walked over to inspect them.

Suddenly, she cried out, "She's here! Her dun quarter horse with our Rafter G brand is tied to the rail right over there!" She ran from the stable and started walking fast up the road. The rest followed, leaving their horses behind. The marshal caught up with Sandra.

"Slow down, ma'am," the marshal cautioned. "We gotta figure this thing out. Accordin' to the stableman, she's up the street in thet hotel, above the mercantile. Her and four men. Thet's their horses tied next ta Miss Lacey's."

They stopped walking and Braddock said, "Seems to me the best thing to do is catch them by surprise."

The marshal replied, "Thet won't be easy, from what the stableman told me. He said they stay close to Lacey. They'll use her fer a shield." He turned to Garnett. "Any ideas, Garnett?"

"Not right off," Garnett replied. He turned to Pruitt. "How about you, kid, you got any ideas?"

"Sure," the young cowboy said, "I got an idea."

"I figured you would," the marshal said sarcastically. "Well, out with it. We ain't got all day."

"We flush 'em out like rats!" Pruitt said enthusiastically.

The marshal laughed. "That's real funny, but this ain't no time ta be jokin' around, kid."

"I ain't jokin' around, Marshal, I'm serious," Pruitt replied.

The marshal gave Pruitt a withering stare. "How you gonna git 'em all out on the street, huh? Tell me thet!"

"It's easy," Pruitt said with a grin. "Heck, we're standin' here a-wastin' time an' a-jackin' our jaws." He looked at Mrs. Garth. "Ma'am, would you come with me, please?"

"Where are we going, Mr. Pruitt?"

"We're goin' up to thet hotel an' git yer little girl back, ma'am."

"Do you have a plan, Mr. Pruitt?"

"Well, sort of, ma'am. You'll jest have ta trust me on this."

Braddock scowled at the cowboy. "I don't think so, kid. She's not going anywhere with you. Especially in there."

Sandra Garth stared into the young cowboy's eyes, trying to figure out what he was up to next. Finally, she nodded and said, "Alright, Mr. Pruitt, I'll trust you."

As Pruitt and Sandra Garth started walking up the street, Braddock grabbed his arm and jerked him to a stop. "If anything happens to Mrs. Garth or her daughter, kid, you're dead. I want you to know that right now. Do you hear me?

"Sure," Pruitt replied with an angry scowl, "I hear ya, Braddock."

"It's alright, Sloan," Sandra said.

"Are you sure, Sandra?"

"Yes."

Braddock sighed. "Well, I think you're making a big mistake."

They followed the young cowboy and Sandra up to the mercantile, and stood at the hitching rail for a moment watching people come and go. No one seemed to take notice of them. They looked like tired, dusty travelers and nothing more. Sandra Garth got some curious glances because of her fancy clothes.

"What's next, kid?" Garnett asked.

"Yeah, kid, what's next?" the marshal said sarcastically.

"You all wait here. Mrs. Garth an' me are goin' in. When I come a-runnin' out, git ready ta do some fancy shootin'."

Braddock growled, "Pruitt, you're crazy!" He turned around to stare at Sandra Garth. "Don't listen to him, Sandra. He doesn't know what he's doing! He'll get you killed!"

Sandra looked over at the young cowboy again. "Are you crazy, Mr. Pruitt?"

"I sure am, ma'am, crazy as a fox," Pruitt replied. "But if you want yer little girl back, you'd best follow me."

Pruitt walked up on the porch of the Crown Jewel Hotel, Bar, Beanery and Mercantile, stopping to look back at Sandra Garth. She stared up at him with a conflicted look on her face. He held his hand out to her. Braddock moved, blocking her path. "Don't do it, Sandra!" he said desperately. "Please don't!"

She stood frozen for a moment then said, "I have to, Sloan. I have to." She walked around Braddock and up on the porch steps alongside Pruitt. She smiled weakly at him, nodded and followed him into the mercantile. The others watched from the street.

Once inside, Pruitt stopped Sandra a few feet inside the door. "Jest wait here, ma'am," he said.

The cowboy walked up to the counter. An old man sat there on a high stool. "You want a room for you and your mother?" he asked, noticing Sandra.

"We're a-lookin' fer my cousin Sally. I hear she's a-stayin' here with my Uncle Tom an' some friends."

"A girl, you say?"

"Yeah, my cousin Sally."

"Thet must be them up in room eight an' ten."

"Are they in?"

"Yup, they jest came back from dinner."

"Thank you, sir," Pruitt said. He walked back to Sandra. "Ma'am, you wait here until you see me and them four sidewinders come down those stairs over there. Stay here with yer back to 'em so they don't notice you. Then go upstairs an' git yer little girl."

"Are you sure this is going to work, Mr. Pruitt?"

"It could, with the good Lord a-willin' an' a little prayin'."

Pruitt turned and walked up the stairs. When he got to the top, he stopped to look at the numbers on the doors. He continued slowly and quietly along the hallway until he came to room number eight. He carefully put his ear against it, listened for a few seconds and then knocked.

"Who is it?" someone asked.

"Me."

"Whatta ya want, 'me'?"

"There's four men down on the street waitin' to send you all ta hell."

Pruitt heard rapid footsteps and the door swung open. He looked into the barrel of Mason's gun and stepped back.

"What was thet you said, ya little piss ant?"

"There's four half drunk fools out in front. They said they wanna brace you an' yer friends. Thet is, unless you all are yellah."

Mason shoved Pruitt further back into the hallway. Downy and Meany walked from the room to join him. Pruitt could smell the stink of alcohol on them. Their eyes were red and glassy from drinking.

"What's goin' on?" Meany asked.

"This little runt says there's four drunk cowboys down in the road a-waitin' ta brace us."

"Is thet so? Well, you go down an' tell them fools we'll be right there, kid," Downy said.

As Pruitt started off, Meany stopped him. "You say there's four of 'em down there?"

"Yep, four half drunk cowboys. They said they're gonna kick yer asses over the girl ya got stashed away up here."

Downy smirked. "They said thet, did they?"

"They sure did. I ain't kiddin'."

Meany said, "Let's get the boss in on this. It'll even things up, four ta four."

"Yeah," Mason replied. "I'll go tell him." He knocked on the door of room ten. "Hey, boss, come on out a minute! We got somethin' goin' on here!"

The door opened and Kinsey Blue came out. Downy spoke first. "This kid says there's four fools down on the road waitin' ta brace us."

"Four?" Blue asked.

"Yep!" Pruitt said. "Thet's right, there's four of 'em."

"Who the hell are they?"

"Jest some half drunk cow punchers who heard about the girl," Pruitt said casually. "They said they wanna take her dancin'."

Blue stared at young Pruitt for a moment, then smirked. "Alright, kid, go tell them fools we're on the way down." He chuckled and turned to the others. "Hell, this should be fun. I ain't been braced in a long time. It's gonna feel damn good ta drill somebody again."

Downy, Mason and Meany chortled. Blue quickly locked the door of room ten and they followed Pruitt down the hallway. He hurried on ahead of them to the stairs and down into the lobby. As he passed Sandra Garth, he whispered the word, "ten," and then was gone. She turned away just as Blue and his men hit the bottom of the stairs in a rush. They glanced at her then kept going. Once they were gone, she immediately hurried upstairs.

Out on the porch, Pruitt and the outlaws stopped to look down at Braddock, Marshal Fargo and Garnett.

"I thought you said there was four of 'em, kid," Blue said.

"There are," Pruitt said as he ran down the steps into the road to line up with the others. "I'm the fourth!"

A crowd quickly gathered on the plank sidewalks to watch what looked like the beginning of a shootout.

"You tricky little sidewinder," Blue growled. "I'm a-gonna fill you full of lead!"

The four outlaws hurried onto the road and lined up facing Braddock, Garnett, Marshal Fargo and Pruitt. About forty feet of muddy road separated them.

Downy chuckled. "This should be easy."

"Yeah," Meany said. "They don't look like much."

Blue positioned himself over to the left, facing Pruitt. "I want thet little shit. He set this up ta get the girl. He's gonna die first."

Pruitt stared hard at Blue. He yelled out, "Did you touch thet girl, mister?"

"Maybe, maybe not. You ain't gonna live long enough ta find out, kid!"

Kinsey Blue went for his gun. It was halfway out when he realized the young cowboy had already fanned off two shots. Pruitt's first shot took Blue in the chest and the second hit him in the heart. The outlaw's body whirled like a top, and went rolling in the road until it stopped faced down in the mud.

Downy and Meany each got off a shot at the same time. Downy was a tad faster, but was off target as his bullet grazed Braddock's left shoulder. Braddock's bullet smashed into the outlaw's neck. Downy sat down, dropping his gun and holding his neck as blood gushed between his fingers. Braddock shot him again in the chest, knocking him flat.

Meany had shot at the marshal but missed hitting him in the head by an inch. The old man turned sideways, extended his arm, calmly took aim and thumbed a single shot into Meany's heart. The outlaw's body shuddered and shook for a moment, then crumbled face down in the mud.

Garnett, shooting from a crouch, fanned off two quick shots at Mason, catching him with both bullets before he even got his gun out. Mason coughed loud as his body went flying through the air as if slapped by a giant hand. He landed on his back, sliding in the mud for about six feet before coming to rest in a puddle.

The crowd stood frozen and awe struck. They had never see anything like this before.

As all this was happening, Sandra Garth found room number ten on the second floor of the mercantile. She put her ear against it and listened. "Lacey?" she said softly. Then again, louder, "Lacey!"

"Oh, God! Mom, is that you?"

Sandra drew her gun and pointed it at the doorknob. "Stand back, baby!"

After firing a shot that shattered the knob, Sandra shoved the door open. Lacey ran into her mother's arms. They held each other, crying and laughing, stopping only when they heard gunfire down below. It was rapid, loud and short and then went quiet.

"What was that all about, Momma?"

"That's what we'll have to find out, honey," Sandra said cautiously.

Sandra Garth held her gun ready as she started down the stairs with her daughter. They stopped at the door a moment, and then went out onto the porch to see who was alive. When she saw the results, she looked up at the sky and said softly, "Thank you, Lord!"

She walked down to Garnett, Braddock, Pruitt and the marshal and hugged them all, crying and laughing for joy. The long, agonizing journey was over. Everything was fine now. It had ended well.

"Thank you all," she said. She turned to Pruitt and hugged him hard. "Thank you, Mr. Pruitt. God bless you." She noticed Braddock holding his arm. "Sloan! You're wounded! Let me help you!" She went over to Braddock to look at his arm.

"It's nothing," Braddock said. He glanced over at Lacey Garth. "So this is your Lacey, is it? She's beautiful."

Lacey didn't seem to hear a word he said. She was staring at young Pruitt as he stood there with his mouth open, catching flies. They were sizing each other up and liked what they saw.

"Let's get out of here," Braddock said, and they headed back down to the stables.

Chapter 10

They were getting ready to leave the Snake Pit. Sandra Garth was attending to the wound on Braddock's shoulder when Marshal Fargo sniffed loudly to get everyone's attention. They stopped whatever they were doing and gathered around him.

"What's up, Marshal?" Braddock asked.

"I think we're forgettin' something," the old lawman said.

"What would that be, Marshal?" Sandra asked.

"The money them sidewinders stole from the Easton's Corner's Bank. If any of it is left, it must be back there in the hotel."

Garnett said, "It would most likely be in Blue's room, wouldn't it?"

"It is," Lacey said. "It's in one of Blue's saddlebags. Under the bed. Room ten."

The marshal turned to Braddock. "You stay with Mrs. Garth and Miss Lacey. The rest of us will go take a look."

Braddock nodded and said, "Sure, be glad to."

Pruitt, Garnett and the marshal walked quickly up the road toward the hotel. Sandra, finished with dressing Braddock's wound, turned to Lacey and said, "This is Mr. Braddock, darling. He's been very helpful and kind."

"Howdy, Mr. Braddock," Lacey said.

Braddock touched the brim of his hat in a salute, and then reached out his hand. "Glad to meet you, Lacey," Braddock said smoothly staring at the young girl. "Are you alright? I mean, did they hurt you?"

Lacey replied with a sneer, "They roughed me up a bit, but not too much. I'm okay. Thanks for asking, Mr. Braddock." They shook hands.

"Please call me Sloan, Lacey."

"Sure. Where you from, Mr. Braddock?"

The question surprised Braddock. He quickly concluded this girl was nobody's fool. She was tough. Only a tough girl could have survived what she had gone through for the past days.

"I'm originally from Dallas, Miss Lacey," Braddock replied in answer to her question.

"Whatta you do for a living, Mr. Braddock?"

A bit embarrassed by the tone of her daughter's voice and her line of questioning, Sandra Garth cut in. "Mr. Braddock is a businessman, darling."

"That's nice," Lacey said flatly. She walked over to her horse and began gently rubbing its neck, whispering to it. It gently nudged her with its head. Suddenly she grabbed the reins and swung up into the saddle.

"Where are you going, honey?" Sandra asked.

"Back up there, to the hotel, Momma."

"Why?"

"They might need some help finding the money." Lacey got her horse headed up the road at an easy gait. Sandra and Braddock watched her go.

Sandra smiled. "She always did have a head of her own." She turned to stare into Braddock's eyes. "I was worried about you, Sloan."

"You were?"

"Yes."

Braddock stepped in close to her. "Can I kiss you, Sandra?"

"If I said no?"

"Then I wouldn't."

"Alright then, don't," she said, softly.

Braddock leaned down and kissed her gently on the mouth.

"I said no, Sloan," she whispered coming up closer to him.

"You were lying," Braddock said and kissed her again.

She stared up into his face. "Alright, do what you want," she whispered.

Braddock grabbed her up into his arms and kissed her once more. She sighed and leaned against his chest.

"I knew it all along," she finally said.

"How?"

"By the way you looked at me. I felt it."

"I know you did." Braddock kissed her again and then whispered in her ear. "How far?"

"As far as you want."

"What about your husband?"

"He's in Kansas City doing whatever he wants."

"So, you do what you want?"

Sandra pulled away. The spell was broken. "I've been a faithful wife, Sloan," she said. "No other man has ever touched me."

He felt deep inside she was not lying. "I believe you."

"We have to be careful. I don't want Lacey hurt. She thinks her father walks on water."

"We'll be careful," Braddock replied.

He took her hand and led her over to an empty stall. The stableman was busy somewhere out of sight in back. They stayed there until they heard voices and a horse coming down the road, then straightened their clothes and hurried out to meet them.

Garnett and the marshal were walking in the lead. The old lawman carried a pair of saddlebags. Lacey came on foot behind them, leading her horse. Pruitt walked by her side. They smiled and talked, enjoying each other's company. Youth connected with youth, shutting out everything else.

"How much did you find?" Braddock asked the marshal when he and the others reached the stable.

"Fifteen thousand was all thet was left. Only half of what was stolen," the marshal replied. "It's here in Blue's saddlebag, still in the sack with the bank's name on it."

"What about the other saddlebags? We should check them," Sandra said.

It took a few more minutes to check the rest of the saddlebags. They found nothing of value.

"Let's hightail it outta here," the marshal said.

They paid the stableman and in a half hour they were on the road heading north towards Sharon Springs, a small caravan of six riders, four outlaw horses, and Sandra Garth's packhorse.

They stopped to make camp when it got too dark to ride, ten miles east of Sharon Springs. In the morning, they headed east again and rode into Coldwater Springs that evening. After a good meal, they stayed overnight and went on again in the morning.

When they came to the wide, raging stream where the barge concession was, they discovered that a man, his wife, and their two daughters had taken it over. They wondered about this, but didn't stop to ask questions. Anyway, it was much cheaper to cross this time. Garnett used the same money he had taken from the previous owner to pay for their crossing. He dropped the rest of it into the pail as they left. The man blessed him.

Later down the trail, they speculated about who the new owners were but never came up with anything that made sense. The best they could think of was they were relatives or friends of the man Garnett had killed.

Marshal Fargo and Garnett watched with interest the game played by Lacey Garth and Rick Pruitt. It was a wonder to behold. He attended to her every need. At night, he cut tender pine boughs for her bed and carried her water. Once he even shot the head off a rattlesnake that offended her by being five yards away.

For her part, she stared down her cute little nose at the young cowboy, demanding more and more attention. He had, in short time, become her willing servant and enjoyed every moment of it. All he got in return was a smile and a touch of her hand on his, which left him blushing. Just the sound of her sweet voice brought him running. The truth was that Lacey Garth was better at the game than Pruitt. She had played it before. Not so for the young cowboy. This was his first time in love, and he had no idea how the game was played.

They stopped at Johnson's Slough to eat at the beanery. This time they kept clear of the saloon. After a hearty dinner, they picked up the three horses that belonged to the tracker Pete Lowry and the other two men from Easton's Corners. Garnett and Pruitt tied them behind the packhorse with the four outlaw horses, and they took to the road again. Easton's Corners was only a few days away. The weather favored them as they made slow, but steady time.

On the last day of their journey Marshal Fargo cornered the young cowboy just before dark, out of earshot of the others. The old man had a serious look on his face

"What's up, Marshal Fargo?" Pruitt asked.

"Look, son, I don't know how ta tell ya this, but yer barkin' up the wrong tree."

"Whatta ya mean?"

"Yer howlin' at the moon, kid. It's daylight an' ya can't even see it." The marshal's voice was pained.

"What?" The young cowboy had no idea what the marshal was trying to tell him. "Fer cryin' out loud Marshal, jest say it out straight, won't ya!"

The marshal let the words rush out. "Lacey Garth is promised, kid!"

Pruitt looked stunned. His face clouded over. "Promised?"

"Yup. She ain't up fer grabs."

"Promised to who?"

"To young Wim Varney."

"Who the heck is Wim Varney?"

"He's the eldest son of Elijah Varney, owner of the Circle V Ranch."

The marshal watched the young cowboy's Adam's apple move up and down as if he had swallowed sand and his mouth had gone bone dry.

"Yep," the marshal went on, "Lacey's dad has it all arranged fer when she turns eighteen, in a month."

"But, she likes me, Marshal!"

"It don't matter. It ain't goin' nowhere, kid. You can't have her."

"Shucks, thet ain't right!"

"Right or wrong, that's how it is."

Pruitt looked like he was going to cry. The old man patted him on the shoulder and walked away, leaving him to wallow in his misery. He found Garnett sitting on a windfall smoking.

"How'd the kid take it?" Garnett asked.

"Like he was kicked in the gut by a mule."

"He'll get over it. We all do," Garnett said.

"Well, if I was Wim Varney, I'd walk a big circle around the kid or he'll git his behind full a lead." The marshal looked around. "Where's Braddock?"

"Find Mrs. Garth and you'll likely find him, too, Marshal."

The marshal looked over to where Lacey was brushing down her horse. "They're getting' mighty careless, I'd say. I hope Lacey never finds out."

Later they all sat around the campfire. Easton's Corners was only fifteen miles away. It would be their last night together. Later, after they had eaten, the marshal said his piece.

"Well, I'd say this sure was one heck of a trip, folks. I'll have ta make out a report that will read like one of them phony Wild West magazines." He looked sadly into the flames of the campfire. "The awful part was we lost some good men. Pete Lowry was a fine tracker. The other two men from town all had families. It ain't gonna be easy ta tell their kinfolk what happened to 'em."

"Yeah," Pruitt said. "You sure can't tell 'em they died in a bawdy house."

"No, I'll write they died in the line of duty," the marshal replied.

Mrs. Garth spoke up. "I'll see that their families get five hundred dollars each from the bank."

"Don't forget about the horses," Garnett reminded the marshal. "Their families will want them back." The marshal nodded.

Braddock cleared his throat. "You can also give them my part of the reward money, Sandra. It's not much, but it's the least I can do."

"That's very nice of you, Sloan," Sandra replied.

"Heck," Pruitt said. "Why not jest give them those four outlaw horses, too? They could sell them fer quite a bit, figurin' in the saddles an' all."

Braddock said, "Since I'm kicking in my part of the reward money, I'd like to swap horses and take Blue's chestnut mustang, if it's okay?"

No one argued against it. They all nodded in agreement.

They sat in silence sipping coffee and chewing beef jerky. Not wanting to appear overly intrusive, they stole glances at each other on the sly. After all, they didn't know each other, and yet, in a way, they did. There was a hidden pride in knowing that they had survived an awful ordeal. They had gone through dangers together that they would never go through again with anyone else, or ever forget. Like it or not, there was a bond between them. But tomorrow it would be broken and shattered as if it had never existed. Each one would go on their way and not look back.

Finally, the marshal yawned. "I'm turning in."

"Yeah," Garnett said. "Me, too."

Pruitt went and cut some pine boughs for Lacey Garth. She stared at him, but he avoided her eyes. The marshal's words were still burning in his mind.

"What's the matter?" Lacey asked.

"Nothin'," he muttered and went to cut pine boughs for his own bed.

She walked over to him and stood looking on as he worked. "You've been very kind to me, Richard," she said.

"Rick. My name is Rick," he said sharply.

"Alright, then, Rick," she replied. "You have been very kind to me and I appreciate that. You're a real gentleman. I wish you luck on your life's journey."

"Thank you, ma'am," he said, as if she were a stranger.

"I'll miss you."

"No, you won't. You'll have Wim Varney to keep yer mind off me,"

"No. I'll always remember you." She turned to go but suddenly spun around and grabbed his arm. She stepped in close and kissed him softly on the mouth.

"Don't you ever forget me, Rick Pruitt!" she sobbed and then went away into the shadows.

Pruitt walked slowly over to his horse with a confused look on his face. As he untied his bedroll, he suddenly realized he would never be able to figure women out no matter if he lived to be a hundred and fifty. He also wanted more of those kisses from Lacey Garth.

In the morning, they discovered that Braddock's horse was there, but Blue's chestnut mustang with the star on its forehead, and the saddlebags with the fifteen thousand dollars, were gone.

"I reckon he liked Blue's horse an' saddlebags better than his own," the marshal chuckled. "It was probably faster, it bein' an outlaw horse."

"Let's go after him, Marshal Fargo," Pruitt said enthusiastically.

The old man shook his head. "No. You go ahead, kid. I'm too tired ta go chasin' anybody right now. I jest wanna git back ta my old bed. Braddock kin go plumb ta hell fer all I care."

"You gonna let him git away with thet fifteen thousand?"

"Yep. An' I hope he chokes on it," the marshal relied.

Garnett glanced over at Sandra Garth. She was staring off into the distance, her face turned away from the others so they couldn't see the look on her face. He noticed the knuckles of her right hand were white as she clenched the handle of her gun tightly in anger.

Chapter 11

They rode slowly and quietly into Easton's Corners late on a Friday afternoon. One or two townsfolk waved at Sandra Garth and Marshal Fargo. No one noticed the weary travelers as they stopped at the stable, and left the extra horses there to be cared for properly.

"Take good care of them, Dan. They need a good goin' over. Check their shoes, too. We'll be back to get them during the week," the marshal said.

"Okay, Marshal, I'll be sure ta do thet," the stableman Dan Cooper said, glad to get the extra business.

"Thanks, Dan."

They rode up to the jailhouse and stopped. The marshal dismounted and tied up at the rail.

"We'll meet during the week and sort things out, Marshal," Sandra said.

"Alright, Mrs. Garth," Marshal Fargo replied.

Sandra turned to look at Garnett and Pruitt. "If you two will come with me to the bank, I'll see you get the money you have coming." There was a coldness in her voice. It was as if she were angry at them, or they were complete strangers.

"Sure thing, ma'am," Garnett replied with half a smile.

As the marshal went into the jailhouse, Sandra led off and the two fell in behind her. Lacey rode alongside Pruitt staring at him, all the while holding back her tears. The young cowboy stared straight ahead, trying not to see the pain in her eyes.

When they got to the bank, Sandra and Lacey dismounted and tied their horses to the rail. Lacey turned to give Pruitt a soulful look then walked into the bank with her mother.

"She won't be comin' out, will she?" Pruitt said to Garnett.

"I expect not, kid. I don't think her mom will let her."

In a few minutes, Sandra Garth came out with the reward money in her hand. She had a hard look on her face as she handed Pruitt his share. He stared at it for a moment, then touched the brim of his hat in a farewell salute. "No thank you, ma'am," he said flatly.

Turning his back on her, the young cowboy rode slowly down the road towards the jailhouse. Sandra Garth frowned as she watched him ride away. "What's wrong with Mr. Pruitt, Mr. Garnett?" she asked, raising her eyebrows. "Doesn't he want his money?" A sarcastic smile formed on her lips.

"I reckon not, ma'am," Garnett replied. "And I don't, either."

Sandra's face clouded over and took on an angry, condescending look. "And why not, Mr. Garnett?"

"I guess you'll have to figure that one out for yourself, ma'am," Garnett replied as he turned his horse to leave.

He followed Pruitt back down to the jailhouse. They both tied up at the rail and went in. Marshal Fargo was at his desk. They stood watching as he wrote on a piece of paper. Finally, he looked up and spoke.

"I'm gonna put out a wanted notice on Braddock. I'll git the bank ta put a five hundred dollar reward on him."

Suddenly the marshal laughed and settled back in his chair with a big smile on his weathered face.

"What's so funny?" Garnett asked.

"Braddock. He sure was stupid."

"How's thet?" Pruitt asked.

"Heck, she was looking for a lover on the side. He coulda been the lucky one. He coulda lived high on the hog."

"I'm not so sure about that, Marshal," Garnett said. "She's a man eater. She'd ruin him for good, training him like a dog. He did the smart thing. He took the money and ran. Maybe he had her figured out."

The marshal chuckled. "Yeah, now that ya mention it, maybe yer right. On the other hand, maybe not. We'll never find out, will we?"

"You can forget about that flier, Marshal. He's probably headed for Coldwater Springs or the Snake Pit by now. The gambling is good there and there's no law," Garnett mused.

There wasn't much more to talk about. "I expect she paid you two," the marshal said.

"Oh, sure, she paid us and kissed us goodbye, too," Garnett chuckled.

The marshal gave Pruitt a sympathetic look and sighed. "It hurts bad, don't it, kid?" he said. "But it's all part of life. You'll look back one of these days an' laugh about it. Especially after ya been kissed by a few of them painted ladies."

Pruitt forced a weak smile. "Yeah, I reckon," he replied.

Garnett looked around the jailhouse and shrugged. "Well, Marshal, this is where I say adios, old timer. It sure was a pleasure."

The marshal stood up and shook both their hands. "I gotta admit it, but you two were the best pards a marshal could ever have. You both were with me all the way. Without you two we never woulda gotten Miss Lacey back." He turned to the young cowboy. "She owes you her life, kid, an' she darn well knows it. An' so does her mother. They owe you big."

"Thanks, Marshal," Pruitt replied. "Thanks. Uh, what about that posse money?"

"Oh, yeah. I guess I owe ya both a hundred and fifty dollars each."

After getting the money from a small, battered safe, the marshal walked outside with them and watched as they mounted up. They turned their horses and rode east, stopping once to wave back. The old marshal stood looking until they were too far away to see. He sighed and, with a sad look on his face, went back into the jailhouse.

Ten miles east, the two travelers came to a crossroads and stopped. Garnett reached into his shirt for the makings and began rolling a cigarette. Pruitt looked at the distant horizon where the westering sun hung above the top of the mountains. The bottoms of the low hanging clouds above them looked to be on fire in the evening light.

"I guess this is it, kid," Garnett said. He lit his cigarette and exhaled a whiff of smoke.

A cool wind blew across a nearby field. Garnett leaned over and rubbed the big appaloosa's neck. It snorted.

"Winter is comin'," the young cowboy said.

"Yeah. I can smell it already, kid."

"Where ya headed, Garnett?"

"South to Ellsworth, then on to Caldwell, I guess. How about you?"

Pruitt stared at the crossroads a moment. "North, I suppose. Up towards Colby. Maybe Stockton."

"Ya gonna wrangle agin?"

"I'm thinkin' on it."

They made small talk until Garnett finished smoking. Crushing the stub out between his fingers, he opened it up and let the unburnt tobacco scatter in the breezes. He reached over and shook the kid's hand.

"Watch your back, kid."

"You too."

They saluted each other and rode off in their opposite ways. Pruitt headed north, and Garnett headed south. When he was a few miles on, Garnett heard a horse pounding up the road behind him. He stopped and turned his horse to see Pruitt riding fast in his direction.

"What's the matter?" Garnett asked as Pruitt reined up beside him.

"I got an idea." The young cowboy seemed excited.

"What's that?"

"Let's go find Braddock and get that fifteen thousand dollars."

"Then what?"

"Thet money belonged to the bank. I bet Marshal Fargo is putting a wanted flier out on him right now. We'll git it first before some bounty hunter does, an' bring it back to the bank."

"How the heck are we gonna find him, kid?"

Pruitt thought about that for a moment. "He's a gambler by trade, ain't he?"

"Yeah, so what?"

"Where's the next biggest town along the trail?"

"Oakley?" Garnett replied.

"Oakley is north. He ain't headed north," Pruitt insisted.

"What makes you think that?"

"He likes big towns. He'll ride south to Scott City, then Garden City and then cut east to Dodge."

"You think he's gonna go all the way to Dodge City to play cards when he's got fifteen thousand to spend?"

"I'm guessin' he'll stop at those three places just to spread a little cash around. He likes to act important with the ladies. I know how his mind works."

"Scott City is about thirty miles south on the coach road," Garnett said. He sat staring down the road where it stretched into the distance. "We're on the coach road now?"

"Thet's right," Pruitt replied. "All we gotta do is follow it south ta Scott City."

"What if he ain't there?"

"If he ain't there, then he went on ta Garden City. We've got a good chance a-catching him either there or at Dodge," Pruitt said. He paused a moment then went on with, "Unless you jest wanna ride on. If so, I'll do it myself."

Garnett stared at the young cowboy. "You're doin' it for her, aincha? It's all for her, ain't it?"

Pruitt shrugged. "I reckon. I guess I wanna show her I just ain't no dumb cowboy."

"You sure must love her something bad, kid."

Pruitt fell quiet. He looked conflicted and lost, as if he couldn't decide which way to go. Garnett watched him as he turned his horse and rode south. He had gone a good way when Garnett rode fast to catch him.

"Changed yer mind, Garnett?" Pruitt asked.

"I'd hate to see you get bushwhacked, kid," Garnett replied. "I'll go along and watch yer back."

"Thanks, pard."

"My pleasure, kid."

They rode on. It was late in the afternoon when they loped into Scott City. It was a thriving cow town with three saloons. They checked each one and didn't find Braddock. Finally, they went down to the stable and talked to the owner.

"We're looking for a friend," Garnett said. "He's ridin' a chestnut mustang."

"Did it have a star on its forehead?"

"That's the one."

"Yeah, I seen a fellah like thet. He came past last evenin'. I usually keep an eye on who comes an' goes around here. He weren't no cowboy. Wore a city suit."

Garnett replied. "That's him, alright. You've got a darn good eye, old timer." The old man chuckled, proud of himself. Garnett gave him two bits.

He and Pruitt rode off, heading further south for Garden City. Two hours later, darkness caught them on the open road so they cut across a field of wild clover that led into a stand of silver aspens. On the other side, they found a suitable place to camp beside a stream. After tossing their bedrolls, they dropped their saddles and gear, brushed down the horses and then hobbled them in a grassy place near the water. Pruitt made the coffee fire, and they ate some jerky and hardtack.

Later, they lay on the ground on their blankets with their heads on their saddles. The sky above them was a vast, bottomless sea. Its huge dome changed color from a dark blue in the east to a warm orange in the west where the sun was sliding down behind the distant hills. The air was cooling down. A breeze came across the field to them, carrying with it the sweet, pungent scent of sage.

"How come ya never got married, Garnett? Pretty soon you'll be so ugly no gal will have ya."

Garnett knew the kid was still hurting from the way Lacey Garth had treated him. "She was the one, wasn't she, kid?" Garnett asked. Pruitt didn't answer for a while. The hurt was too deep.

Pruitt sighed then said, "Yeah, I reckon she was. But the marshal was right, she's outta my reach."

"If you think she's outta yer reach, then she's outta yer reach." Garnett replied. He began to build a cigarette.

"What's thet supposed ta mean?" Pruitt asked.

"It means if you want her you gotta go after her, kid."

"How the heck am I supposed ta do thet? She has book learnin'. I kin hardly read."

"Seems like there ought a be a way," Garnett said.

Pruitt replied emphatically, "Garnett, there ain't no way, an' you darn well know it."

"You keep thinkin' like that, kid, and it'll get you no place."

They fell silent for a while, staring at the shadows cast by the dying campfire. Finally, Pruitt said, "If anything happens ta me, Garnett, make sure they bury me with my saddle and tack, won't ya?"

"There ain't nothin' gonna happen to you, kid."

"An' set my horse free, too, won't ya?"

"Sure, kid, whatever you say."

"An' you kin have whatever money I got."

"Sure, I'll be rich."

"An' I wanna be buried by myself, not in some boneyard next to a bunch a drunks. Like out on a hill, where it's lonesome, someplace."

"Sure, sure, kid, if that's what you want," Garnett said, half asleep.

"Ya promise?"

Garnett heard the urgency in the young cowboy's voice and said, "Sure, kid, I promise."

They left it at that, saying no more as the fire died down. Wrapped in their blankets, they stared above. The sky was full of diamonds that twinkled on and off into the night. They pulled their hats over their faces to shut out the world. Coyotes howled in the nearby hills. Garnett lay most of the night trying to think of a reason to get Pruitt to give up the hunt for Braddock. He fell asleep without thinking of any.

Chapter 12

They got an early start the following morning and rode into Garden City around noontime. They made inquiries at the hotel and saloon and found no trace of Braddock. After that, they sat in a beanery drinking coffee and trying to figure out their next move. Garnett wanted to give up the hunt.

"There's no sense in goin' any further," Garnett said. "Braddock coulda turned north or south. We've got no way of tellin' for certain."

"I still think he's headed fer Dodge," Pruitt said. "Let's keep goin'. It's a fifty mile ride an' we still might catch him."

"Yer whistlin' in the wind, kid," Garnett said. "Let's give it up." He suddenly had a bad feeling about this. It felt as if a cold winter wind had descended upon them.

"We've come too far now, Garnett," Pruitt replied with enthusiasm. "Come on, let's go! We're getting' close. I kin feel it."

Garnett sighed in resignation. As much as he wanted to turn back, he didn't want to abandon the young cowboy. They followed the main road heading east, out of town. As they got to the end, Garnett saw an old man sitting in front of a stable alongside the road. He was whittling away on a piece of wood while he gummed a chew of tobacco. Blue's chestnut mustang with the star on its forehead stood tied to a rail out front. The saddle, saddlebags, and other tack were gone.

The two men stopped. Pruitt pointed at the horse. "See that, Garnett?" he asked.

"I sure do," Garnett replied. "I sure do, kid."

The old stableman looked up at them and spit a stream of brown tobacco juice on the ground. He noticed how they stared at the horse. "Nice mount, ain't he?" he said proudly. "Ya kin have him fer five hundred."

"Where'd you get him?" Garnett asked.

"A feller sold him ta me this mornin'. He's a beauty, ain't he?"

"He sure is," Garnett replied.

"Ya wanna buy him?"

Garnett deflected the question. "Did the man say anything?" Garnett asked.

"Nope."

"Which way did he ride?" Pruitt asked.

"He didn't," the stableman said. "He took the stage to Dodge. Took his saddle and tack wif him."

"Thanks, ol' timer," Pruitt replied. He turned to Garnett, yelling, "We got him now, Garnett, let's ride!"

Without waiting, Pruitt urged his mount into a rapid gait. Garnett caught up with him, and they rode together with their mounts stretching out and biting the wind. They were ten miles out when they heard the sound of gunfire up ahead.

"What the heck's that about?" Pruitt asked Garnett.

"Sounds like a gunfight is going on!"

A quarter of a mile more and they came to a left turn in the road. The noise got louder. As they rode around the turn,

130

they saw a stagecoach about twenty yards below where the road sloped and then leveled out. Garnett and Pruitt walked their horses over into a stand of scrub oaks, dismounted, and tied up. They stood on the rise looking down at the scene.

Six outlaws surrounded the stagecoach. The whip was lying on the road not moving, while the shotgun was crouched down in the front boot firing over the side with a rifle. Inside the coach, someone was yelling at the outlaws to stop firing.

"There's a woman in here!" the voice screamed in a panic.

"That sounds like Braddock," Garnett said.

The outlaws ignored Braddock's plea and kept firing. The gambler poked his arm out of the coach window, and fired off a shot that had no effect. The coach was full of bullet holes.

"The whip is dead," Pruitt said. "He's a goner!" Just then, the whip rolled under the coach and into the ditch on the other side, out of sight. "He was only playin' possum, I guess," Pruitt said.

"We'll have to take 'em from here, kid," Garnett said.

Pruitt yelled, "Heck, let's go down there and kick their scuzzy butts!"

"That's not a good idea, kid," Garnett said. "They'll see us coming."

"Yeah? Well, jest you watch. I'll show ya how a cowboy does it!"

Before Garnett could stop him, Pruitt pulled his Colt and ran down the slope. Garnett grabbed his rifle from its saddle sheath, got down in a firing position and levered a round into the chamber. The young cowboy was about a hundred feet from the coach when one of the outlaws saw him coming. Pruitt stopped running and fanned off a shot. His bullet hit the outlaw in the chest, knocking him flat on the road.

Two of the outlaw's companions saw what had happened, and turned their guns on Pruitt. Garnett shot one in the chest and Pruitt shot the other one in the heart. When the remaining three outlaws realized they were being blindsided, they all turned and fanned off a fusillade of bullets at the young cowboy. Garnett levered off shot after shot, trying to cover Pruitt as he ran straight into the oncoming lead.

Garnett groaned and cursed as he saw Pruitt go down on one knee. Even then, clutching his chest, the young cowboy thumbed off a round, taking out another outlaw. He kept firing until his Colt was empty and he fell sideways into the field, near the road. Garnett levered off a final fusillade of bullets that knocked the last two outlaws flat on their backs. When the dust settled, all six outlaws lay dead in the road. Pruitt's motionless body lay in the field.

The stagecoach door swung open. A woman climbed out, rushed to Pruitt and knelt beside him. She put her arms around his shoulders and cradled him in her arms. Garnett dropped his rifle, grabbed his canteen and ran down the slope. When he got to Pruitt, he pulled the cork and handed the canteen to the woman. She held it to the young cowboy's mouth. He took a short drink and groaned.

The woman started to cry. "I saw you, cowboy. You were wonderful."

Pruitt's eyes sparkled. He stared up at Garnett and forced a smile. "See, Jesse, thet fortune teller was right, wasn't she? It's jest like she told me. I'm a-dyin' in the arms of a beautiful woman."

"Yeah, pard, it looks like she had it right all along," Garnett said softly, his voice breaking.

Pruitt let out a long sigh, the light went out of his eyes and he fell limp in the woman's arms.

"Oh, God!" the woman cried out as she held the young cowboy close, rocking him back and forth.

Garnett left her and went to check on the whip who was just climbing out of the ditch. He was winged in the side. The shotgun climbed down from the box, holding his shoulder.

"Friend," the shotgun said, "I don't know how to thank you."

"Who else is inside besides the lady?" Garnett asked.

"Jest some gambler. I think he's a-dyin'."

"I'll see if I can help him."

Garnett stared into the coach. He saw Braddock slumped back on the seat, holding his chest. Blood ran between his fingers and bubbled from the corner of his mouth. His eyes were glassy. The saddlebags lay on the bench beside him.

"Is that you, Garnett?"

"Yeah," Garnett answered, opening the coach door, "it's me, pal. The lady, is she with you?"

"I wish she was," Braddock replied, trying to smile. He coughed and then recovered. "Pruitt...I saw what he did. The kid is a real cowboy. I gotta give him that."

"He was the real thing," Garnett replied.

"The money...it's here, in the saddlebags."

As Garnett glanced at the saddlebags, he heard Braddock let out a long sigh. When he looked back, he saw the gambler was dead. Garnett left him, took the medicine box from the front boot and attended to the driver and guard. He worked fast. Their wounds weren't bad enough to stop them from functioning. He went to the woman. She sat looking down at Pruitt, sobbing.

"Do you mind riding with a dead man, ma'am?" Garnett asked.

She looked up at Garnett. "Please, I'd rather not."

"Alright."

Garnett and the guard pulled Braddock's body out of the coach and laid it alongside the road. Garnett helped the woman back into the coach.

"Thank you for saving my life," she said to Garnett.

"You were lucky you didn't get hurt, ma'am."

"That man, he made me get behind him. He was a real gentleman." She covered her face with her hands, and started to cry some more.

"Yeah," Garnett replied, "he was a real gentleman."

"I'll pay for his funeral in Dodge City," she said, "It's the least I can do. My husband is well known there."

"That would be nice, ma'am."

"I'll take the young cowboy, too."

"I'll see he's taken care of, ma'am. He was my pard," Garnett replied. The woman nodded in understanding.

Garnett grabbed Braddock's saddlebags and closed the coach door. He went to speak with the whip. "I'm taking the saddlebags. Before he died, he said I could have them. Any objections?"

"Heck no, friend," the driver replied. "You saved our lives. Take it."

"The lady wants to pay for the gambler's funeral in Dodge. Can we load him on top?"

"Sure."

"Then let's do that now."

After they had lain Braddock's body on top of the coach, Garnet asked the whip, "What about the outlaws?"

"What about them?"

"Take their guns, horses, saddles, and tack. There's lots of money there, if you two want it. We'll drag the bodies over in the field for the coyotes and buzzards."

"Seems like a good plan," the shotgun replied.

"Let's do it an' get the heck outta here," the whip said urgently.

Garnett slung the saddlebags over his shoulder and walked wearily back up the slope. He laid it over his own saddlebags, tied it fast with the latigos and then put his rifle back in its sheath. Grabbing the reins of Pruitt's horse, he led it down the slope.

When he reached the bottom of the slope, he saw that the shotgun and the whip had taken the outlaw's guns and gunbelts and put them in the saddlebags on the horses. They were now dragging the bodies over into the field. While they were busy with that, Garnett tied the outlaw horses to the back of the stagecoach. All this time the woman sat mournfully crying inside.

"Good bye, ma'am," Garnett said, standing by the door but not looking in at her.

"Good bye. I'm so sorry about your young friend."

"Thank you, ma'am. So am I."

The whip gave Garnett a shovel and an old, soiled, worn wool blanket from the boot and thanked him for all he'd done. He and the shotgun climbed up in the box and the stagecoach moved off with the six outlaw horses in tow. Garnett stood alone in the road watching it go out of sight. A sad look came over his face as he lifted Pruitt's body, and laid it over the saddle of his horse. Forcing back his tears, he picked up the shovel and blanket, grabbed the horse's reins and walked slowly up the long slope to where his own horse was.

Garnet found a small clearing in a cluster of scrub oaks and went to work digging a grave. It was hard work and it took a long time, but by late afternoon he had dug the hole deep enough. Wrapping the young cowboy's body in the blanket, he lowered it gently down into the hole. He took the saddle from Pruitt's horse and placed it and the other tack over Pruitt's legs. Finally, he laid Pruitt's hat on his chest.

He stared down one last time with a sorrowful look before shoveling dirt back into the hole. When it was full, he smoothed the gravesite out and packed it down with the shovel. With that done, he covered it with dead branches, weeds and grass, then hid the shovel in the brush. Finally, he climbed on the bare back of Pruitt's horse and nudged it at a walk down the slope to the field. Once there, he slid off the animal's back and stood by its side, talking to it and stroking its neck.

"Yer pal is gone now, fellah," he said, his voice cracking with emotion. "Yer pal is gone. Go find a new one."

Garnett slapped the horse hard on its left flank. It whinnied and bolted off into the field. Halfway across, it stopped a moment to look back, then ran on, free as the wind. Garnett walked slowly back up the slope. He was numb with emotion and completely exhausted. Sitting with his back against a scrub oak, the ex-outlaw rolled a cigarette and stared off into the distance, trying to picture Pruitt's face and his friendly smile. He knew in time it would fade away, but for now he wanted to keep it clear in his mind, along with the sound of his voice and manner of talking. All the things that made him who he was.

It was getting late and the shadows were long. It was time to go. Before riding off, Garnett checked Braddock's saddlebags. He was surprised to find not only fifteen thousand dollars of the bank's money, but another five thousand as well. Garnett figured Braddock must have been lucky at the poker table in Garden City. Maybe those six outlaws had seen him win big and followed the coach to rob him. He didn't have Warfield, Wheeler and Preston around to protect him anymore.

Garnett decided to take the five grand as a finder's fee. He put it in his saddlebags with the eight thousand already there. Suddenly, the prospects of buying a small business looked much better now.

Three days later, dusty and tired, Jesse Garnett rode into Easton's Corners and tied his horse in front of the jailhouse. He got Braddock's saddlebags and walked inside. Marshal Fargo was going through some wanted fliers. When the old lawman saw Garnett, he broke out smiling, got up and shook his hand.

"The kid said to give you this, Marshal," Garnett said, dropping the saddlebags on the lawman's desk.

"What's this, the kid's saddlebags?"

"Nope, it's the one Braddock stole, the one with the bank money."

"Well, I'll be danged! Where's thet young wildcat?" the marshal asked. "Did he ride off ta shoot Wim Varney an' kidnap Lacey Garth?"

"Not hardly." Garnett told the marshal how Pruitt and Braddock died.

The marshal looked sad and nodded. "Yeah, thet sounds like somethin' the kid would do."

"Once he told me he was gonna die in the arms of a beautiful woman," Garnett said. "And darn if he didn't. Can you figure that one out?"

"Nope. Not if I lived ta be a hundred years old."

The marshal dumped the money out of the sack onto his desk and counted it. When he was finished, he put it back in and said, "I'll drop this off at the bank."

"You can keep the saddlebags. Braddock won't need them anymore."

"Thanks." The marshal shoved the saddlebags in the bottom drawer of the desk. He stared at Garnett. "You look frazzled."

"Yeah, I'm tired and hungry."

"Go up to Becker's Beanery and have some of his chili. It'll do ya good."

"That sounds like a plan," Garnett said.

The marshal picked up the money sack and he and Garnett stepped outside. Garnett grabbed the reins of his horse and they walked slowly up the road. When they got to the bank, the marshal turned off.

"I'll see ya up at the beanery," he said as he headed into the bank.

"I'll be there," Garnett replied.

He continued up the road to Becker's place, and tied his horse at the rail. Once inside, he took a table by the window. Becker came over. Garnett ordered chili and crackers. He had two bowls of the salty stuff and washed it down with black coffee. Rolling a cigarette, he smoked and waited for the marshal.

As he sat there, Lacey Garth came riding slowly down the road with a young man. She glanced into the beanery window and saw Garnett. A look of surprise came over her face. Quickly reining her mount to a stop, she said something to the young man and he rode on. She hurriedly tied her horse to the rail, and rushed in to join Garnett.

He started to get up, but she stopped him. "Please don't get up," Lacey said. She stood behind a chair at the table, looking around the room as if searching for someone.

As Garnett sat back down, the marshal walked in. "Hello, Miss Lacey," he said, as he took a chair at the table. "Garnett brought back the money thet Braddock done ran off with."

"Oh, how wonderful," Lacey replied, smiling. She continued looking around. "Where's Mr. Pruitt? I don't see him. He's with you, isn't he?"

Garnett looked down at his coffee cup for a moment then shook his head and sighed. "Miss Lacey, Rick Pruitt is dead, ma'am."

Lacey Garth looked stunned. Her smile faded and she grabbed the back of the chair for support, clutching it tightly. "What did you say, Mr. Garnett?" she asked, her voice cracking.

"He's gone, ma'am."

There was a long silence as the young girl looked out of the window and then around the room as if searching for Pruitt. Garnett saw disbelief in her eyes.

"Did he tell you to say that, Mr. Garnett?"

"No, ma'am, he didn't. He's dead."

She stared hard at Garnett. "Well, then, how did he die?" she asked harshly.

"Like a cowboy, ma'am. Saving someone's life."

Lacey slowly moved around the chair and sat down. She fought to hold back the burning tears that were trying to burst forth. "Tell me what happened to him. I want to know."

Garnett nodded. He told her everything, even about burying Pruitt in a grave on a lonely hillside over thirty miles away. Lacey began to cry hard. Tears streamed down her face, and her body shook in agonized jerks. Looking up at

Garnett, she cried out, "God is punishing me for treating him so badly!"

The old marshal looked away, not knowing what to say.

"He loved you," Garnett said. "If it helps any, he loved you enough to die for you." He stood up and put some money on the table. "I'll be going now, Miss Lacey. Give my regards to your mother."

Garnett shook the marshal's hand and left. They watched him go. When he was outside, about to mount up, Lacey rushed out and grabbed his arm. "Show me where he's buried, Garnett, please!"

"There's no reason for you to go there."

"Please!" Lacey begged.

Garnett looked down at the young girl. "You should let it go, Miss Lacey. Hang on to who you thought he was and what you imagined him to be. Think of him as a cowboy who loved you with all his heart. Hold on to that, if you can. It's all you'll ever have of him now."

"I loved him!" Lacey cried out. Tears ran down her cheeks. "I loved him and I never told him!"

Garnett reached out to her and she came into his arms. He held her gently and said, "I think he knew it."

Garnett mounted up. Lacey softly stroked the neck of Garnett's horse. "Braddock loved my mom, didn't he?"

"If he ever loved a woman, I expect it was her," Garnett replied.

"Well, she never loved anybody but herself," Lacey said scornfully.

"I'm sorry to hear that, Miss Lacey," Garnett said sadly. He stared at Lacey Garth one last time. "Goodbye, Miss Lacey."

"Goodbye, Mr. Garnett," Lacey said, wiping her tears. "And thank you for everything."

Garnett followed the road leading east out of town. When he came to where the roads crossed, he headed south. The land opened wide before him, full of colors, smells and sounds. Birds darted about overhead. Higher up, a lone eagle wheeled about in wide circles, dark against the cotton clouds. Its wings looked like sails, keeping it afloat on the currents. It seemed to be waiting for him. He looked up and nodded.

"Alright, darn it, I'm coming. Don't rush me," he chuckled.

Jesse Garnett rode south. Riding with his thoughts, he realized he had nearly thirteen thousand dollars stashed away in secret pockets of his saddlebags. He almost had enough to start that little business he dreamed about. All he needed was a new suit and a woman to share his dream with.

The End

STAGECOACH TO BREMER'S ROCK

Excerpt

Preston's face was red with anger and his eyes narrowed. He pointed a finger at Garnett. "Mr. Larson, I seem to be having a problem here. I'd like it if you or one of your men took care of this saddle tramp. Do it quickly, please. I want him out of the way so we can take care of the business at hand."

Larson looked over at Garnett and then at his men. There was a look of indecision on his face, as if he wasn't sure what to do next. Finally, he asked, "Any you boys wanna do it?" He waited. No one moved or spoke up.

When the rancher realized that no one cared to take his offer, he said quickly, "I'll give a hundred dollars to anyone who puts a bullet in this fool."

It was a few moments before someone took the offer. "Hell, for a hundred, I'll do it," someone said.

A tall, lean cowboy wearing his black hat low and chewing on a matchstick climbed slowly down from his horse and walked over to a clear spot away from the others.

He turned to face Garnet with a casual smile on his lips, his hand down by his gun, his legs braced. He took the matchstick from his mouth and let it fall onto the ground.

WESTERN BOOKS BY R. ANNAN

Fight for the Lazy M
The Red Bandana
The Salvation of Trace Logan
The Cowboy from Sierra Blanca

Jack Cordell Westerns

The Gunfighter in Winter
Long Ride to Hell's Kitchen
Owl Hawks
Gunfight at Barfield Springs
Shootout at Sanctuary City
Last Days of a Gunfighter

Clay Jared Westerns

Copperhead Moon
Cowboys of the Box R
Prisoners of Brimstone Pass
Range War in C Minor
Devil Wind
Showdown at Wamego Falls
Lightning Riders
Winter Kill
Gunfight at Wild River
Shootout at Rattlesnake Flats

Jesse Garnett Westerns

Gunfight at Black Bear Lair
Gunfight at Latigo Junction
Outcasts of Troublesome Creek

Look for other books to appear soon!

ABOUT THE AUTHOR

As a young boy growing up in the city, R. Annan never passed up a chance to see a western movie. His heroes were Buck Jones, Johnny Mack Brown, Wild Bill Elliot and John Wayne, to name a few. As an adult he often wondered where his love of westerns came from. Perhaps it has something to do with his grandfather, John L. Annan, who was a cowboy from Helena, Montana, in days of old.

R. Annan is a seasoned and traveled author with many interests. As a career serviceman, he served in Korea and Vietnam. He also completed a one-year course at the Defense Language Institute in Monterey, California, and graduated from the University of South Florida with a B.A. in Art and Art History. After taking a two-year course in screenwriting at the Hollywood Scriptwriting Institute, he established The Old Time Radio Club Time Machine as both a scriptwriter and an actor.

A Note from the Author

Thank you for reading my book. If you enjoyed it, would you please consider rating and reviewing it? I'd enjoy your feedback. Thank you!

www.ingramcontent.com/pod-product-compliance
Lightning Source LLC
Chambersburg PA
CBHW070931130626
46555CB00001B/379